Kanook Kibbutznick

.

Kanook Kibbutznick

Mike Hoover

2007

Kanook Kibbutznick

Acknowledgments

Special thanks to Victor Sherman, Santa Monica, California. Richard Farrant and Mike O'Rielly for standing tall and not giving in to the mob. Cdr. John Hough, U.S.N. Ret., and his wife Sally and family, Annapolis, Md., who took me in and treated me like one of their own. Gerry Hough, who was my big brother when I needed one. Michael Sherwood, U.S.M.C. Ret. The best first mate I ever sailed with. Mike Morningstar, Parkersburg, W.Va. The staff and students of Glenville State College, Glenville, W.Va. I'm still waiting for my honourary degree. James Allan Jones, Detroit, Mich., America's greatest Shakespearian actor and scholar. Elizabeth Mansour, Vancouver, B.C., who took me to all the football games when I couldn't afford a ticket. Jessica Murphy Oliver, B.C., for all her help and encouragement. R.C.M.P. Constable Don Wigglesworth, who told me I was a very talented writer. R.C.M.P. Sgt. Kevin Schur, who told me I should find a new hobby. Mel Greenberg, Queens, New York, who talked me into flying El Al. Gil Posner, Keats Close, London, England. The kibbutznicks at Yotvata and Hamadiya. The Kettle Valley Railroaders. Tamore Tukhala, Penticton, B.C., and David

Lynch, Oliver, B.C., for getting this all started. Bruce Isaacson. Martin Abramson. David Abramson (thanks for inviting me to your bar mitzvah). Laurie Ukelson. My lawyer, Howard Rubin (I didn't forget I still owe you money).. Gracie Flannagan (Gracie's Place, Queen Charlotte City, B.C.). Bob Bull, who tried to teach me grammar, Dan West, Jody McElligot, Athabasca Alberta. Lorna Rissling, Cover art design by John Churchman Writers Retreat Okanagan Valley

Dedicated to my Aunt, Theresa Berdine-Cole who sent her husband, Sgt. Sherman Cole U.S.A.F. Ret., 365 letters while he was serving in the Republic of South Vietnam in 1968—69. You are in our prayers.

Kanook Kibbutznick —My life in the Mossad

Chapter One

Penticton was a railroad town when I came into this world. The old Penticton Hospital where I was born has now been turned into an old folk's home, and that's where I intend to end my days. I have decided that I want to go out where I came in. Everybody I tell that story to says I'm crazy. You can be the judge of that.

One of my grandfathers worked at building the new hospital. He was a carpenter and an American citizen and left with my grandmother to go back to the United States to build a dam on the Columbia River, leaving my mother in Penticton to marry my father. I grew up as a Canadian citizen but, like many Canadians, I spent a fair amount of time south of the border.

My other grandfather was a Canadian and he sold everything from cars to real estate. I don't remember it, but the SS Sicamous, a Canadian Pacific paddle-wheeler, used to dock at the lower end of Main Street. The SS Sicamous plied the waters of Okanagan Lake from Penticton to Okanagan Landing north of Vernon. There is an old Indian legend of a lake monster called Ogopogo who is still supposed to haunt the lake, and my Canadian grandfather used to make a lot of jokes about the ridiculousness of the legend.

Grandfather was an avid fisherman, and one day while out fishing he saw something that startled him and put an end to his fishing days for good. Many years later, just before he died, he admitted to seeing something in the water that seemed to fit the description of the lake monster.

Not far from where the SS Sicamous used to tie up, the Kettle Valley Railroad's Penticton station was located. The train used to stop in front of the Incola Hotel, a magnificent structure that made an imposing site looking north onto Okanagan Lake. When my father was a boy, he and his friends would take turns diving off the pier and swimming around the ship as she was docking, much to the consternation of the captain and crew. The Kettle Valley Railway and the SS Sicamous were the lifeblood of the Okanagan Valley, and my father got his chance to work on the railroad after World War II when he returned from fighting the Germans for six years.

My parents raised us kids up in a classical world. My father was a very good opera singer and when the Kettle Valley Railway changed over from steam to diesel and he lost his job, he packed the family up and moved us from Penticton to Vancouver. I was pretty young but I remember heading out in our old Dodge with the mattress on the roof, past Dog Lake as they called it then, and out of town. Our first stop was the old Richter Ranch, where we stayed overnight and left our kitty cats. Then it was over the old Hope-Princeton highway and down into Vancouver. My father had an audition with the Vancouver Opera Society shortly after our arrival and when he passed the audition it was opera, opera, opera, and more opera.

Our regimen was a little unorthodox. My father bought an old RCA record player and a set of opera records for (if I remember correctly) Pagliacci, and the opera was on. My brothers and sisters and I would come home from school and get into character. When Father arrived home from work the record would drop, the arm would travel across the old 33 1/3 vinyl, the needle would fall, and a scratchy symphony would begin and we would take to the stage and the show would go on. By the time I was six or seven I could sing the entire score of Pagliacci by heart, in Italian. We were allowed to go to the dress rehearsals at the Queen Elizabeth Theatre and were quite a sight—and sound—singing word for word with the stars from our place way back in the balcony.

My father, who wasn't classically trained, was selected to be the understudy for one of the lead roles. He looked upon it as his chance for his big break. Father found himself understudy to the great Robert Merrill who had somehow found time to leave the Metropolitan Opera in New York and sing with a small opera company way out on the west coast of Canada. This man was a huge star, world renowned. Father brought him home one day and it was like being in the presence of a god. We were allowed to do our show for him and he was polite but we were working-class people and he was like royalty. The great Robert Merrill never got sick or broke a leg, and Father's chance for the big break came and went. My brothers and sisters and I, on the other hand, were still required to sell our souls to the devil hundreds of times, as is required in Goethe's Faust.

While this was going on, the weekends were another matter. On Sunday Father would pack us off to the local Catholic church for high mass. We had to learn the entire mass; this time, however, it was in another language—Latin. At the time I grew to hate this inculcation but it would really pay off later in life when I would have to learn another language just for survival.

All of us kids were installed in a Catholic private school which was a couple miles walk from home. Along the way we had to pass by a public school, and one day some of the Protestant boys started shouting out that the priests were screwing the nuns. In my mind I assumed a classical character and became so enraged I decided it was my duty to defend Sister Mary Margret's honour. I took a real beating that day and I still have the scar where my eye almost popped out. However, I wasn't to be outdone. When I was healed up enough I found a package of matches somewhere and stopped by their school on the way home from my school. I gathered up some gum wrappers and other paper lying around and started a fire next to a door and I still remember pushing it up to the door with the intention to burn the place down. It wasn't long before the janitor came out and put out the fire. I thought I made a clean getaway but I think my blue corduroy trousers, white shirt, and red bow tie kind of gave me away.

The next day at school two Vancouver City Police officers, who seemed to be the biggest, scariest uniformed men in the world, escorted me, one per side, out of my grade three classroom and into a waiting police car for the proverbial ride downtown. With Sister Mary Margret watching the proceedings and the rest of my classmates burrowing their noses into their notebooks, I was definitely on my own. I think the reason they didn't cuff me was that my wrists were too small. I was on my way to my first visit to 312 Main Street, and it would be thirty years before my return.

The city jail was located in the oldest, most rundown part of Vancouver, and the officers pulled up in a dark lane behind the jail where prisoners are brought to be processed. We were joined by other policemen who were bringing in their own prisoners and they joked back and forth about the little arsonist. Even though I didn't understand the word I got the meaning. We rode up the elevator with other prisoners who were all in cuffs. When we reached our final destination, I was marched into an office and seated on a chair. After a while, being too afraid to ask to go to the washroom, I proceeded to wet my pants. This didn't go over too well with my captors and one of them screamed at me for messing the chair I was sitting in. I thought it was just the thing to do because from where I was sitting I could see into a holding cell and a prisoner in there had pissed his pants also.

My parents were horrified when they got the call from Sister Superior that I had been hauled off to jail and subsequently had to come down to 312 Main to bail me out. As it turned out, I was much too young to be charged, and the officers just wanted to scare me a little and see what kind of family I came from. I told them the story of the fight with the Protestant boys and showed them the scar but it wasn't enough to convince them that I had done the right thing. When Father and Mother showed up at the jail they were spared the humiliation of coming into the cells area. I was delivered to them, wet pants and all, in the lobby of the building. It was a very quiet ride home. But that all changed when we went into the house. Father got his belt out and gave me a really serious whopping and sent me to my room to think about what I had done. I felt a little like a hero betrayed.

I decided that the boys who beat me up so bad had to be paid back. I knew where they all lived and I knew their routes to and from school. So I planned to get them one at a time. The first kid was easy; he was much smaller than me and I got him on the way home from school one day. I caught him alone and I beat him senseless and it made me feel good. The second kid is where my plan failed. I saw him after school and chased him all the way home. When he made it into his yard and felt safe, he began to mock me so I picked up a rock, threw it at him, and nailed him in the left temple. I saw him fall to the ground and roll around doing "the Chicken." I didn't wait around.

I must have thought I was safe because I remember being quite surprised when the next day Sister Superior removed me from the classroom and brought me into her office. Sitting in her office this time were two Vancouver City Police lady officers, both my parents, and the bishop. I instantly thought that I had killed the kid.

I wasn't the only boy called up on the carpet that day. I had already been ratted off by other members of my papist revenge squad. William Bader, who was a grade below me but one of the boys I would walk to school with, had already been interrogated and pleaded his innocence. What my mother told me when we got home was that Billy's interrogation had been anything but ordinary. What they didn't know was that Billy had a pet white mouse that he kept secret from Sister Superior. When the sister came to retrieve Billy, he didn't have time to put the mouse anywhere else so he just stuffed it down his pants. When the interrogation got underway Billy started squirming and fidgeting and when the mouse started chewing on Billy's pecker and he couldn't take it any more he pulled down his pants and out popped the mouse. Well, I guess Sister Superior almost jumped out of her skin, the bishop harrumphed, and the cops followed the sister's lead and began screaming. It was chaos in the principal's office. My mother told me it was the funniest thing she had ever seen.

When it was my turn to stand before the assembled inquisitors and go through an interrogation it was beginning to be apparent that I was formed out of a different mold than the rest of the students. I tried to explain that these Protestants were all going to hell anyway so what did it matter. I didn't get any arguments about my philosophy from the nuns or the bishop; the lady cops, however, wanted to take me downtown. Somehow my parents got into the conversation and I was given a reprieve. The nuns thought that I had been somehow adversely affected by the operas. The bishop was in agreement but my father, who only went to church to sing and didn't care too much for religion anyways, wanted to remove me from the school. There was no argument from the nuns.

In the end they all agreed about my punishment. They removed my desk from my classroom and hauled it down to the gymnasium and said I had to stay there for a week and pray for guidance from the Holy Spirit.

I was only down there for a couple of hours when the janitor came by and started to make these long sweeps back and forth from one end of the floor to the other with this large broom. After a while he looked up at me, and at the same time removed a package of cigarettes from his coveralls, stuck one in his mouth, and offered me one. I had never smoked a cigarette before but accepted his offer anyways. There was a big pile of chairs beside the stage and he took two down and arranged them for us. We sat down and lit up. I was feeling pretty good. Old Mr. Stevens seem to understand my predicament and sympathized with me.

We were having a good time talking and puffing on our cigarettes when Sister Superior appeared out of nowhere. She wasn't too impressed. She was there to deliver a message: the bishop was waiting to hear my confession and I was to follow her over to the church. I took one last drag on my smoke, butted it out, and followed her out of the gym.

When we arrived at the church I was escorted into the confessional and I started out with the usual "Bless me, Father, for I have sinned." I was used to being called a little arsonist by now, but how I got mixed up in the confessional is beyond me.

The bishop replied "Yes, my son, what are your sins?"

And I said, "I have committed adultery."

The bishop screamed, "With a married woman?"

And I said, "No, with Billy Bader."

All I remember after that was hearing his door slam and mine open. He was a big man even if I was just a child. He picked me up and began to shake me. My mother, who was present, began screaming at him to let me go. I remember her shouting at him, "It's a good thing you never got married because no woman could stand to live with you!" It was total chaos and I didn't even know what adultery was, let alone how to commit it.

Things got straightened out after a while and I must have been told the difference between the two sins because I have stayed away from arson ever since.

Our routine didn't change much until one day Father got a chance for a real paying job in an opera. It was to be performed in New York City. This was a dream come true for Father. It was not only with a big famous opera company, it was the show he had always wanted to be a part of. The opera was Othello. He had waited all his life to sing Othello, the opera that meant something quite different from all the other operas he had been a part of. This one took him back to his Kettle Valley Railway days and the trip down the Coquihalla Canyon.

When the builders of the rail line that linked Penticton with Hope named the line stations they used Shakespearian names, and the tragedy Othello played a big part with names like Iago and Romeo and the Othello tunnels. Father had been steeped in this play and used to quote from it every trip up and down the canyon. He would often talk of how he knew the World Champion Penticton Vee's hockey team and how some of them worked with him on the rail line and how they all loved riding through the Othello tunnels. He talked about the players with reverence and how they were responsible for putting Penticton on the world's stage. He was so excited to study this opera, he made us not only memorize the Italian, but also had us learn the Shakespearian version. We spent even more time than usual practicing both versions. When we saw Father off at the airport we didn't realize that his career would keep him away from home for the next few years.

My brothers and sisters always had good grades and I was just the opposite. Sister Superior tried to beat learning into me with the strap. She strapped me so many times that my hands were a mess, but I kept up my crazy behavior. She would call me up at night and always ask the same question, "What am I going to do with you?"

Of course I would reply, "I don't know." I know what I wanted to say but never had the guts to say it. I think back on it after all these years, this stupid bitch calling me up almost every night with the same question. Then at the end of the school year she was sent back to Toronto and everyone said I had driven her to a nervous breakdown. Me, the guy who had stood up for her when she was being maligned by those Protestant boys! I saw myself as a hero and a defender of the faith when in the eyes of everyone else I was a problem child.

Father's singing career was on the decline when he came home for good; he just showed up one day and informed us that we were moving back to Penticton, the place of his youth. My mother was selling real estate by now and she was to open an office and Father was to begin chasing his first love: being a cowboy. They had purchased some land and he was going to turn it into a ranch. Our classical life ended that day and the strange life of a small town took its place.

The very first day I arrived in Penticton I met some boys in the local pool hall. They were getting some beer and invited me along. We found a local man to act as our bootlegger and we received the beer and proceeded to drink it under a bridge until we were drunk. That was my first epiphany—I had found the thing I was looking for. Up to this point I had never had a drink in my life but now that changed forever. I was an instant alcoholic. Booze gave me the confidence I didn't know that I had lacked. Liquor was going to be my passion for the next couple of years.

In order for us to survive, Father had to commute to Vancouver to his job and that left me on my own. Starting her real estate business took up most of my mother's time, and I went wild. My grades at school were horrible and I didn't make many friends. Getting drunk and getting into fights turned out to be my best subjects until I was finally kicked out of school for good. It was generally decided that I would join the army and see if I could be taught some discipline.

At that time, my uncle was in the U.S. Air Force stationed in a place called Bien Hoa, Republic of Vietnam, and my aunt volunteered to take me in and take me to the recruiters. She lived in Tacoma, Washington, so I was placed on a bus and sent south. Years later when a friend of mine who was teaching school in Penticton looked up my school records, he had to laugh. It said, "He's gone to join the army, if they'll have him."

CHAPTER TWO

I remember pulling into Seattle on the Greyhound bus and looking up at the Space Needle and being very impressed—seventeen years old and without a clue. Life at my aunt's house in Tacoma was very structured. She had three kids to raise and there were always lots of other women coming over to the house whose husbands were serving in Asia, some in Vietnam, some in Thailand. But the one thing in common was the talk of war and the great anxiety they felt for their husbands. It was just natural to be in uniform and my time would come soon enough. Every woman who came to the house, along with my aunt, would write a letter every day to her husband, and if someone missed a day the ladies would get together and write two the next day. I liked the atmosphere and when we drove up to Seattle to the army recruiting office I was really ready.

I helped my aunt pack all the kids into the car for the drive to Seattle. We drove through the downtown area, making the requisite drive by the Space Needle. For the kids it was like a religious experience. After that we parked the car and filed into the army recruitment office for my big day. The office wasn't busy and I walked up to the counter and said I wanted to join the army. There, standing behind the counter with his neatly pressed uniform complete with campaign ribbons and medals, was a master sergeant, and he was only too friendly. He began his well-rehearsed talk, and we had begun to fill out some forms when my aunt spoke out, "Don't forget to tell him you're on probation."

With this the sergeant looked up, stopped filling out the forms, and asked if that was so. When I answered "Yes," he took the forms and threw them in a waste paper basket and said they didn't want anything to do with me.

I turned and headed for the door. But before I was out of earshot I heard the sergeant shout, "Why don't you try the marines? They'll take you today."

Conscription was the order of the day and the draft was in full swing so the army could be very choosy about whom they would enlist, but the marines were a different story. They didn't offer the opportunities that the army did; they were very much combat-oriented. If I joined the marines I was almost guaranteed to be placed in the infantry and sent to Vietnam. "What the hell," I thought and we walked around the corner to the USMC recruiting center and in the door. This time my aunt kept her mouth shut. I was under age so she had to vouch for me, which she did, and I left the office with a bus ticket along with papers ordering me to report to MCRD in San Diego, California, for basic training. I was a United States Marine Corps recruit.

I had one week before I was due to report and the time passed quickly. Then I climbed aboard the bus and headed down Interstate 5 to my new life. When I finally arrived at the reception center I had to stand in line to present my orders, and when my turn came the S1 clerk took one look at my papers and shouted out, "Hey, Sarge! I think we got us a goddamn commie Kanook over here!"

The sergeant made his way over to the front of the line. "Let me see those papers." He then started perusing my orders.

To this day I don't believe he knew how to read English. His name was Staff Sergeant Fernando Mejia and he was a veteran of the battle of Hue where he served with the famous 2/5, and he let us know repeatedly that his platoon was responsible for killing hundreds if not thousands of NVA regulars.

"Where you from, boy?" he asked me in his thick Spanish accent.

"I'm from Canada, sir," I answered, afraid I would piss myself.

"Sir? I work for a living, boot. You call me Staff Sergeant. Now get down and give me twenty-five."

At the time I was so green I didn't know this was all a set-up. The S1 clerk would find some new recruit with something different on his forms and he would call over the nearest DI to put on a little show for all the other scared kids. It worked.

"I'm going to keep an eye out for you, boy," Staff Sergeant Mejia screamed in my face when I finished my twenty-five pushups. As boot camp progressed I grew to hate Staff Sergeant Mejia but the training he forced on me would go a long way to saving my life. His training would also turn me into a very efficient killer of men. It was Staff Sergeant Mejia who started calling me "Kanook." The name stuck for the rest of my time in the corps and even now, when I hear from one of my old war buddies, that is the name I am called.

All of the new recruits had to line up in alphabetical order and march over to another building to draw our gear. We were all getting hungry but we had to line up again and march to our barracks and stow our gear in our foot lockers, and then it was off to the barbers. There was a lot of hurry up and wait that first day and when we were all pig-shaved we were lined up again in alphabetical order and marched off to the mess hall. When my turn came I pushed my tray along the same as the recruit in front of me and the recruit behind me, but when my turn came to be served, out of nowhere there appeared Staff Sergeant Mejia.

"Kanook, you pinko commie motherfucker, you don't like our American chow? Get down and give me twenty-five." I was down doing pushups while the rest of the line moved on.

"Do you know how to stand at attention, Kanook?" shouted Staff Sergeant Mejia. He proceeded to use me as an example for the rest of the training company to demonstrate how to stand at attention. I was on the verge of tears, my sergeant screaming in my face, and the rest of the company afraid to look up from their "shit on a shingle." He finally released me and I tried to make myself invisible but this would go on every day for the rest of boot camp. He would sneak up on me and begin screaming "Kanook, 'aboot' face!" and then march me in front of the other recruits. "Forward march, 'aboot' face, forward march, 'aboot' face!" I was to become his private project, the object of his tyranny whenever he got the chance. His tactics to humiliate me were textbook. The special treatment would make me very hard.

My first day as a marine wasn't even over and it was obvious that I was going to either toughen up or that crazy DI was going to kill me. When we were finally marched to our barracks for lights out I got to meet some of the other kids who were in my training company. I found out we were not that different. Most of us had troubled backgrounds. Hardly anyone had completed high school. There were underprivileged kids from the inner city, and farm boys from Oklahoma. There were miners' sons from Idaho, and there were cowboys from Texas. One thing most of them had in common was a deep sense of patriotism and love for their country—so much so that a lot of them were willing to die for their president. This was all foreign to me. I was there because nobody else would have me. There was an intense hatred of communism and a great longing to kill commies. It all sounded good to me and I was willing to go along with whatever we were told to do and hate and eventually kill.

The next day we were all lined up on the parade ground in formation after a five-mile run learning how to stand at attention and salute. They switched around the DI's so you never knew who you would get from day to day. When Staff Sergeant Mejia got close to our line he shouted out, "I want that commie pinko Kanook to move forward!" I could feel the rest of the recruits cringe as I moved out of the ranks and to the front of the line. "Get down and give me fifty, you pink ass motherfucker!" shouted Staff Sergeant Mejia.

I immediately dropped down to the ground and began to do pushups. I struggled to do the last ten and then stood up to attention. The sergeant screamed at me, "Did I tell you to get up, boy?"

To which I replied, "No, Staff Sergeant."

"I'll Article 15 your ass, boy, if you disobey an order. Now get back down on all fours." He then produced a tin can and placed it in front of me on the ground and ordered me to start picking up the cigarette butts that littered the area. The tarmac was hot and burned my mouth but I picked them up as fast as I could while Staff Sergeant Mejia screamed at me, "Not that one, boy, this one! Now crawl over here and pick up this one! That's a good Kanook." This continued while the rest of the company stood at ease until I was ordered back in the ranks and Staff Sergeant Mejia departed.

Over the next few weeks I came to expect this on a daily basis. I came to sense his presence and cringed when he would appear. I was totally wrapped up in my own personal hell and wished I had never joined up. Some of the other recruits told me to get away when I would come near until I really felt like I didn't belong. I was really happy to fight the recruits who avoided me with the pugil sticks, and I would give it to them with a little more intensity. If Staff Sergeant Mejia was in the area when we were practicing hand-to-hand combat he would usually pick me to spar with, and I would get kicked around like a rag doll. From a standing position he could roundhouse kick me in the head and knock me to the ground in an instant. I learned how to fight trying to defend myself from him. It was really of no use because he was as fast as a cat and mean. He would knock me to the ground and stand with one foot on my throat mocking me.

The day finally came when we were all loaded onto buses and driven to the rifle range. The noise was deafening. We were each issued an old M14 rifle and began shooting at targets. This is where I had one up on most of the other recruits. My childhood friend's father had had an old British .303 rifle with peep sites and we used to go up into the back woods and shoot beer bottles off of old stumps. His father would drink the beer and we would shoot the rifle. I became a crack shot and only got better with the combat rifle. This was the first time I received anything but grief from the DI's. A good marksman was a valuable commodity in the corps. My instructor actually called over some other DI's and complimented me. "That's some good shootin', Kanook," said Sergeant Brand. "Where'd you learn to shoot like that?" Before I could answer he said, "Boy, you gonna git ya some when you get to The Nam."

When Staff Sergeant Mejia accosted me the next time he was sure to add, "So you think'you can choot, you pink assed scumbag." I could tell even he was impressed. As they do in the corps, the DI's break you down and then slowly build you up into their mold. This was the beginning for me. I was on my way to becoming a first-class killing machine.

A few days later I was called into the sergeants' office and was promoted to acting squad leader. This was the proudest moment of my young life. It didn't come without resentment from the older recruits but that didn't matter to me. I reveled in my new power.

Boot camp finally ended and we all received our Military Occupation Specialty; mine along with almost everyone else was "El Rifleman," and my orders were to remain at Camp Pendleton for AIT, Advanced Infantry Training, consisting of learning how to arm Claymore mines, shoot 3.5-inch rocket launchers, 106mm recoilless rifles, flame throwers,

M60 machine guns, throwing hand grenades, and lots of physical exercise. We even loaded up on an old World War II amphibious vehicle and made a beach landing and really played war. That was the most fun of all, yelling and screaming and assaulting a make-believe enemy who couldn't hurt us.

When we finally finished AIT and received our new orders, all the seventeen-year-olds in the company were held back for jungle training while the eighteens and older were transferred to all corners of the earth. Most received orders to Vietnam. Jungle training was intensive; we spent most of the time climbing the hills and valleys around the base, completing more weapons training, and marching and running. We even got some time off and made the trip down to Tijuana where we all got drunk, involved with a Mexican prostitute, and ended up with the clap. When we all discovered we had VD and had to report to sick bay, our sergeants had no mercy on us whatsoever.

After four weeks of jungle training I reached my eighteenth birthday. My present was receiving orders to be posted to West Pac, a euphemism for deployment to Vietnam.

Soon after receiving our orders we were all loaded up on a bus and driven north past San Francisco to Travis Air Force Base where, sea bags in hand, we departed on a World Airways government contract flight to Kadena Air Force Base, Okinawa. The flight attendants were as friendly as they could be with such a nervous and ribald contingent of passengers. Sixteen hours later we arrived in Okinawa. It was obvious we were getting closer to war. Looking out the window I could see lined up on the tarmac C-130s, Phantom jets, and B-52 bombers with ground and flight crews scurrying everywhere.

When we deplaned and walked into the airport a feeling of anxiety engulfed everyone. There were two kinds of soldiers milling about: the clean-cut new guys and the survivors, the young men on their way home still in there dirty fatigue uniforms, scuffed boots, longish hair, and the "I've been there" look.

Again we were loaded onto buses and were driven to transit barracks where we would remain until our trip "down South." After arriving at our temporary barracks we were given make-work duties of policing the area and generally hurrying up and waiting. We all looked pudgy and overweight compared to the vets who were waiting for their trip back home.

After six unbearable days we were loaded into a C-130 and departed for Da Nang, Republic of Vietnam. I think we all got sick to our stomachs when we spotted land over the South China Sea and descended into our landing pattern. I remember thinking that this really can't be happening; it was all kind of a game up until now, this really can't be happening.

We landed at Da Nang Air Base in our stateside utilities with our "high and tight" haircuts, the epitome of the "newbie." When the hatch was opened we were greeted by a type of heat and a smell that would live with us the rest of our lives—urine, feces, and diesel mixed with 109 degree Fahrenheit heat. After collecting our sea bags we were loaded onto buses with their windows covered with a screen mesh to keep us safe from any kind of grenade attack on our way to the reception center. When we arrived at the center we lined up alphabetically and presented our orders. When my turn came up I was ordered to the Third Marine Division at a place called Phu Bai, about halfway between Da Nang and the ancient city of Hue. At Hue City there had been a fierce battle between the marines and the NVA with which we were very familiar, having listened to Staff Sergeant Mejia in boot camp. There was a truck transport convoy waiting for all the replacements heading north and soon we were on our way.

It was late when we arrived at our new base camp and we were shown where to chow down and given a hooch to spend the night. The next day we lined up at the supply tent to draw our field gear and weapons and to receive our designations.

The next morning seven of us, referred to as a replacement group, boarded a CH-46 helicopter and headed out to the bush. The infantry company we were to join up with had been out on patrol for ten days. They were somewhere up in the hills close to the Laotian border, running what were called aggressive patrols, looking for the enemy. When the helicopter settled down we were rushed out with the mail and supplies and left in a whirl of dust. We were met by a salty gunnery sergeant, and everyone was assigned to a different squad. "You, FNG, report to Lance Corporal Putnam's squad," were the first words I heard upon my arrival in the bush. The platoon was breaking camp and getting ready for the day's "hump." In Canada "humping" meant having sex but in The Nam "humping" meant a forced march up and down hills, through elephant grass, jungle, and wait-a-minute vines; tough slogging in that heat.

Lance Corporal Putnam retrieved me from the landing zone and introduced me to the members of his squad. They all ignored me without even so much as a hello. They were all busy stowing gear, checking weapons, bitching and grumbling, waiting for orders to move out. He took me aside and told me, "Don't you go makin' no noise. If the shit starts, keep your ass down and just keep firing and you'll be all right."

When the order came to "saddle up" one of the squad members named Morgan came over to me and said, "Listen up, cherry. You fuck up and you're on your own. You fuck me up and I'll kill you myself. You're not going to get me killed." I thought I was a tough guy from all my training but that put a shudder down my spine.

We moved out in a long column down the side of the hill where the platoon had bivouacked that night. I had never been so scared in all my life as I mimicked every move of the marine in front of me. We humped all day—the longest day of my life, only to stop for heat casualties and to chow down. Thankfully we found a stream and filled our canteens. Without that water I don't really think I would have made it through my first day in the bush. In the early evening we climbed our last hill and started to set up our night defensive position. Orders came down the line to expect movement but nothing happened that night. The next day was much of the same. In fact it was over two weeks before we had contact of any kind.

After two weeks of patrol, our squad was ordered to set up a night ambush. Lance Corporal Putnam ordered us to travel light, and as the darkness started to fall we slipped away from the platoon and set up our fields of fire next to a huge bomb crater.

It must have been around four o'clock in the morning when someone kicked me awake and said, "There's a Gook in the crater over there. Bring some frags and come with me." It was Morgan, a real hillbilly from West Virginia. He had been in-country for over eight months; a real killer and now he smelled blood. We crawled to the lip of the bomb crater and he tossed a hand grenade over the edge and waited. There was a "harrumph" and a sound of splashing water. It had been raining a lot and the grenade landed in the water at the bottom of the pit, and all that happened was a small concussion but no damage. He tried again, this time holding on to the frag for an extra second with the same result. "Harrumph" and more splashing water but no damage.

By this time the platoon had been put on alert and the mortar men had fired some illumination rounds into the air and we could here the radio squawking, "What the fuck's going on?" while Morgan readied another frag. He held it for an extra second and over the rim of the crater it went; I heard it bounce and again another "harrumph." But this time, out of the far side of the crater, this little guy came up and over the rim, peasant's machete in hand and feet beating down the trail so fast no one even got a shot off.

We returned to the platoon immediately as our position was compromised and got teased for not getting a kill. The captain came down to our position and chewed us out, and as shit rolls downhill everyone blamed me for screwing up their sleep.

For me this hump had been a rough two weeks but the rest of the company had been out for over three weeks with no contact. They were brutal conditions. Hump all day and set up at night, send out ambush teams, and wait. The heat and mosquitoes had been our only enemy to date but that could change in an instant. On my twenty-first day in the bush everyone was getting very edgy because of no contact. There was lots of evidence that there was enemy around us but it was like they were waiting for a battle on their terms.

On the morning of the twenty-second day the lead column spotted a couple of NVA near a stream filling their canteens and opened up on them, killing one and possibly wounding the other. When they moved in to investigate they were met with a barrage of enemy fire. Five marines were killed instantly and several others were wounded. We had stumbled into an NVA base camp. There were 82mm mortars falling on us and we were being raked with 50mm machine gun fire. It seemed like forever before an OV-10 appeared in the sky spraying the area with rockets and machine gun fire. All this time we were putting down as much firepower as we could, but without seeing an enemy soldier.

The OV-10 pulled up and an F4 Phantom screamed in, dropping canisters of napalm. When the first Phantom pulled up another made a pass, then the OV-10 would make a pass expending its ordinance. Finally the enemy fire ceased and I could hear marines screaming and cheering, "Git some, git some." Then the artillery started to pound away at our perimeter; that went on for hours. The OV-10 would make a pass and spot some NVA and then the artillery would respond. This was a day of death for everyone. The medivac helicopters picked up our wounded, our dead, and our dying and we moved in to police up the base camp. Everyone picked up a war trophy that day but it was bittersweet seeing the body bags lined up at the Landing Zone. The company spent the night there and then we were lifted back to base camp the next day.

I had been baptized with fire but my squad still referred to me as a cherry, and until I had a confirmed kill that name would stick; however, I wouldn't have to wait long. We were assigned to guard the perimeter of our base camp. My squad was dug in down by the dump where the sappers were known to infiltrate. Even with that in mind it was regarded as light duty and now there were lots of bennies. We took our turn and everyone that wanted one had a shower. Some of the troops were ordered to have a haircut, which came with lots of bitching. The food was hot and we got to drink as much water as we could and there was also lots of marijuana to smoke; in fact, it was more available than beer. It was really the first time I had smoked and we got all smoked up and sat and watched the fireworks from the outgoing artillery from the army base up Highway 1 a few miles away.

We were not aware of any of the politics that was going on around us but the Third Marine Division was about to be withdrawn from Vietnam and that would include our battalion. It would be a staged withdrawal, but not before we had another trip out into the bush. The short-timers were not happy at all, they didn't want to risk getting killed for no reason but for me I just wanted a chance to "bust my cherry" with a confirmed kill.

After a few days of stand-down the entire company was heli-lifted out to a deserted fire base to see if we could entice "Charlie" into one last battle before re-assignment back to Okinawa and early outs for much of the company. We dug in and waited, sent out patrols and ambushes, but no "Charlie." After no contact for a week my squad was sent out on a patrol leaving the rest of the platoon behind. By this time I was starting to be accepted but I was still a cherry and, with that, still not really trusted. We humped all morning and set up an ambush on a hill when Morgan got really excited. "Gooks, Gooks, see um?" They were so far away all I could see was what looked like a worm crawling way off in the distance. "Here's your chance, cherry," he said to me.

There was a column of NVA working their way toward us, and for a few seconds you could see them and then they would be obscured by the tall elephant grass. They were too far away and out of range for my M16 but Morgan was a real vet and he hated the M16. He carried an M14, which was heavier and didn't have the output, but was much more accurate at long distances. He handed me his weapon and I was shaking like a leaf. He was as excited as me but he had been through this many times and it was like a ritual to help me "bust my cherry."

"Now take a deep breath, and wait until you can get a clear shot," he said. Then he said, "Pop the first one in line and then we'll call in the arty." I took a deep breath and then another. The wait was excruciating. I didn't think I would ever get a clear shot. At that distance I had to judge the "Kentucky Windage" and the pace that the lead soldier was walking. It wasn't going to be easy; they would move and stop, then proceed with caution. Then I got my chance. As the enemy soldiers walked out into the open, I fired my weapon. The distance was so far that the report of the weapon was over before the enemy soldier lurched, his arms flying in the air and dropping to the ground. The rest of the column disappeared in the tall grass while our squad leader was on the radio calling in an air strike. We sat back and watched the fire works. Morgan retrieved his weapon from me and said, "Nice shootin', Kanook. It was the first time I had been referred to by anything other than "cherry."

It's hard to explain the feeling of your first kill, but it was invigorating. After the air strike Morgan said, "Oh shit, we've got BDA," meaning bomb damage assessment, and added that we had to make our way to where we had just ordered the air strike and report on the damage. It was a long march and we all had a bad feeling about it. Bomb damage assessment was the least liked mission for grunts. It was never pleasant and lots of times the enemy set up an ambush knowing that there would be marines coming their way. We started down off of our position with the most caution I had ever experienced, just one squad with the unenviable task of making a body count. When we finally reached the area where we had called in the air strike it was not something that you would want to write home about. We were just happy that there was no ambush to deal with. We made our count and left the areas as fast as we could, double-timing it back to where the rest of the platoon was bivouacked. It didn't take long until other members of the platoon came by and congratulated me. Even the captain came by and said he was proud of me. I was finally accepted and it was a great feeling.

Our platoon was not the first to be withdrawn and we went out on two more long patrols before I started turning yellow. One of the grunts named "Yellow Dog" started making fun of me saying I was trying to steal his name, but for the navy corpsman who was our medic it was a different story. He diagnosed me with infectious hepatitis and I was medivaced back to Charlie Med near Da Nang and isolated with about a hundred other marines with the same sickness. The hospital was air conditioned, with clean white bedding and pretty, round-eyed nurses. At first I was too sick to eat, but being able to sleep whenever I wanted was like heaven compared to where I had just been. I spent almost two months recovering, and when I was about to be released I was told that my platoon had shipped out back to Okinawa. I was really upset that I didn't get to see any of my buddies before they left.

In the hospital everyone acted tough and told all kinds of war stories and I became quite a good liar. But I wasn't satisfied, so when an officer came in looking for replacements for a marine recon unit I volunteered. I had almost six months in-country so I seemed like a vet but in truth I had only been in a couple of firefights. After my discharge from the hospital I made my way back up to Phu Bai and to the Third Force Reconnaissance Company and started training for recon. Before I ever went out on a patrol my R&R came up and I caught a flight out of Da Nang to Subic Bay in the Philippines. After being bussed from the airport to marine barracks we all went out on the town that night—hundreds of marines out on the town of Olongapo. This place was one long street of bars that were really just whore houses. I was only there a week before I came down with the clap. Again. Because of my hepatitis I couldn't drink, so I spent all my time screwing the bar girls. It seemed awful funny when I had to line up at sick bay with dozens of other marines with the same problem. R&R went by too fast and before I knew it I was jumping off a helicopter at Phu Bai.

When I was a line grunt all I was responsible for was my M16. When needed, officers would call and control air strikes. In Third Force Recon even the first-class privates needed to know how to do everything in the bush. It was training and inspections, live fire exercises, and team briefings over and over. I became proficient at ordering any element of air, artillery, or naval gunfire for any type of fire support. It seemed that my training took forever, while real teams were going out and coming back to camp. And all I did was train.

Finally, one day our gunny approached me on the chow line and told me to be ready to go out the next day. I was to join a seven-man team being inserted on a mountaintop for seven days and I better be ready for battle. This was not like going out on patrol with the line grunts; there was no steel pot helmet or flack jacket. We were set up to travel light; along with our water canteens we carried M72 shoulder-fired rockets, Claymore mines, explosives, gas grenades, and an M60 machine gun. I didn't sleep much that night. I had to check and recheck my equipment, clean my M16, and generally be ready to muster at daybreak.

The next morning, with all my equipment checked and rechecked, I met with the rest of the team and waited for the helicopters to arrive. When the helicopter touched down, we and the air crew were briefed. A captain from Intelligence told us that it had been reported that enemy activity in the area was on the increase and we were going in to confirm or deny those reports. After our briefing we boarded the bird and lifted off. We were in a CH-34, accompanied by a Cobra gunship. I loved flying in the helicopters. The air was so fresh and cool and the loudness seemed to settle my nerves.

We dropped down and made false insertions on several hills before we landed on our specific LZ. We hit the ground running and didn't stop until we were in the jungle. We grouped and the lieutenant and the gunny oriented themselves with their maps, then the lieutenant pointed and we were off, moving slowly and silently ahead, using only hand signals. Everyone was on the highest state of alert, scanning everywhere before making a move. We didn't stop until just before nightfall when we found a spot that was defenceable, sent out a perimeter sweep, and looked for any enemy signs. The lieutenant called in our coordinates; we chowed down and went to sleep.

I was kicked awake for my watch at 0:300 but I was awake anyway. We slept in a circle back to back trying to put up with the rain and mosquitoes. If you had to take a pee you did it in your fatigues; there was to be no movement that night. I only had to pee once and all I could think about was pissing my pants while sitting in the police station when I was a child. What a contrast and how times had changed! I was cold and wet and scared out of my wits and wetting the bed. The jungle was alive that night with all kinds of sounds; however, none could be attributed to the enemy.

We were on the move at first light. We found a trail and moved parallel to it in the thick jungle trying to step in the tracks of the man in front, all the time scanning in every direction and listening intently. We moved up a valley between two hillocks until we hit the crest where we rested and the lieutenant climbed a tree to get a better read on our position. When the lieutenant came down from the tree his eyes were almost popping out of his head. He said there was a large column of Gooks moving across the other side of the valley in the open and he was going to call in an artillery strike. He was on the radio to the 105 Battery and then climbed back up the tree and waited for the shells to start to fall. In a couple of minutes they were raining down across the valley. He shouted down a coordinate adjustment to gunny, who was on the radio, relaying the info to the artillery.

"Fire for effect," he screamed. The ground shook from across the valley and then we started to receive some incoming small-arms fire. Our position had been compromised and it was time to get out of there as fast as possible. We didn't bother moving parallel to the trail; we just started running for all we were worth.

We kept up as good a pace as we could but we were pursued all the way. They started lobbing mortars ahead and around us as we moved. We stopped once to request immediate extraction and then were on the move again. We passed over the ridge line and down into another valley, across a stream, and up the other side. We followed a trail up to the top of the next mountain and found an old bomb crater and decided to make a stand there, again calling for immediate extraction. By now we could see the NVA grouping at the bottom of the hill on the other side of the stream and we all opened up with as much fire power as we could send out. They were dropping in the water and on the shore line and they started to fire back at us. Dirt flew up in our faces and bullets and tracers were flying over our heads.

"Eagle Six, this is Thunderball. We got boocoup gooners coming across the blue line! Copy?" I heard the lieutenant scream over the roar of the gunfire. The lieutenant had the 105's adjust their fire mission and was calling for an artillery strike at the bottom of the hill. That didn't stop the NVA. They started to make a desperate charge up the hill to get as close to us as they could to get out from under the murderous shells raining down on their position. We in turn killed as many as we could get in our sites. Then an OV-10 Bronco appeared in the sky and made a pass, sending rockets into the area and spraying machine gun fire. Then out of nowhere an NVA soldier popped up and threw a hand grenade up and over the edge of the crater. I fired a burst that sent him flying into the air backwards and that is all I remember. The grenade blew, knocking me unconscious. The team fought hard until we were all extracted. I was thrown onto the deck of a helicopter, given up for dead.

I didn't wake up until I was on the hospital ship USS Sanctuary. I had undergone surgery to remove some tiny metal fragments lodged in my throat and was heavily sedated. It was the first time I had been in air conditioning since my last stay in Charlie Med and I felt as though I would freeze to death. My head expanded almost to the size of a beach ball and it took a couple of weeks for the doctors to get the infection under control. When I was judged fit for service I boarded a flight to Phu Bai and was greeted by the whole company like a returning hero. We had put a serious hurt on Charlie and didn't lose one of the team. I had a nice scar on my neck and a Purple Heart to go with it. I had been decorated by a general in my hospital bed aboard the ship.

My neck wound never healed properly and when infection set in again I was on a medivac helicopter back to Da Nang and rushed to a hospital in Japan. After more surgery I was sent back to Okinawa and from there back to Camp Pendleton and an honourable medical discharge. I was an eighteen-year-old veteran with a Purple Heart and a couple hundred bucks in my pocket.

CHAPTER THREE

I bought a bus ticket and rode the Greyhound back to Canada. Everyone I had hung around with before I joined the service had long hair and was still drinking wine under the bridge. And I still had my "high and tight" U.S. Marine Corps haircut and couldn't get used to living without barbed wire everywhere and not carrying a weapon. It didn't take too long to fall in with the town losers, drinking cheap wine with my little crowd, tripping around town, and staying up all night. It was a ragtag bunch just one step ahead of the law. We never really did anything criminal—we were just too spaced out.

This went on for about a year when I got a phone call one day from Morgan. He was about to take advantage of his GI benefits and attend college in West Virginia. It didn't take much to convince me to join him. I was off again riding the Greyhound south. When the bus stopped at the border and I had to show some ID, I pulled out my discharge papers and was treated like royalty. I felt like I was home. When I had been back home in Penticton I had quickly learned not to mention my experiences because they were just too unbelievable for the locals' little minds. The border official, who was also a veteran, held the bus up for at least an hour and we swapped stories. It was nice to see the power of a uniform again.

After about a week on the bus I arrived in Gilmer County, West Virginia, and was met at the bus by my old buddy Morgan and a few members of his family—they all wanted to see what a Kanook looked like. Morgan's family lived up what was commonly known as a "holler." He seemed to be related to someone in every house we drove by. When we arrived at his parents' house the first thing he did was introduce me to his coon hounds and take me squirrel hunting. We talked about the war and Nam and there was no letting back. War was natural to Morgan; his family had been fighting in one or another for hundreds of years.

Morgan's family were real hillbillies, but far from being unsophisticated. There was a state college in the county seat and most of his relatives had a degree of one kind or another. He took me into the college to take some tests and fill out my GI benefits forms. I was admitted into their program for returning vets. The course was full every semester and even though I only had an eighth-grade education, which truly showed with my test results, they let me into the program anyway.

This was the fall of 1973. I began receiving a check every month from Uncle Sam and attending college. My grades were less than stellar. Then something happened that would change my life forever, again. Just as joining the U.S. Marine Corps was the first big moment in my life, watching television on October 6, 1973, was the second.

On a national news broadcast I heard the newsman describing how the Egyptian army had crossed the Suez Canal at a place they called the "Bar Lev" line and that the Syrian army had attacked a place called the Golan Heights. In response, the Middle East had erupted. Next I saw the prime minister of Israel, Golda Meir, addressing the Knesset. She quoted the Old Testament, "An eye for an eye and a tooth for a tooth."

I had the second epiphany of my life. I was moved beyond words. I couldn't find Israel or Syria on a map, Egypt maybe. I had no comprehension of Middle East politics. I was functionally illiterate on the subject but that didn't matter. I went to Morgan and told him I was going to Israel. Morgan was horrified. "It's not your fight," he told me and tried to talk me out of this craziness. I wouldn't listen and quit college anyway, and with my Canadian passport in hand and six hundred dollars, I said goodbye to West Virginia, to Morgan and his family, and boarded a bus for New York City. I arrived in the middle of the night and caught a shuttle to the airport. New York was like nothing I had ever seen—even in the middle of the night it was crazy.

When I arrived at the airport, the busiest check-in line was for El Al, the Israeli national airline. The majority of the people in line were Israeli reservists who were mostly students and other American Jews who were heading to Israel to volunteer for positions ranging from hospital nurses to farm labourers. I met a kid in line and we hit it off immediately. His name was Gerry Greenberg from Queens, New York. He had been to Israel before and spoke a little Hebrew. I hadn't even thought about a language issue. I just expected that everyone spoke English. I remembered how the Vietnamese spoke a kind of gibberish, but we hardly considered them people.

I had to wait for two days before I was allowed to buy a ticket and then another day before I was allowed to board a plane. I bought a one-year return ticket for around three hundred dollars and was in the air on my way to the Middle East. Gerry and I were on the same flight and he was going to show me the ropes. He had friends on a border kibbutz and we would be accepted as *mitnadev,* farm labour volunteers. I didn't know what to expect, but being a combat veteran I was craving any kind of action. I just hadn't got my fill in Vietnam and felt kind of robbed, having been discharged honourably for medical reasons.

On the flight over I couldn't help remembering my flight over to Okinawa and then on to Da Nang. But the mood on this flight was much different. Most of the passengers would be in uniform within a day of their return and the news reports were not that encouraging. It had been a surprise attack, by all accounts, and took the military and the country by surprise. Also, the attack came on one of the holiest days in the Jewish calendar, Yom Kippur, a word that meant nothing to me. On my flight to Asia there had been obvious fearful anticipation but on this flight soldiers were going home, and they knew exactly what unit they would join, where they would muster, and who they would be fighting. It was a cacophony of Hebrew and although I felt like an outsider, I was swept up in the moment, generating testosterone for the coming battle. In a way, I was going home too.

When we landed Gerry suggested we head up to Jerusalem and stay at a youth hostel until we got our destination sorted out. We happened upon a kind of a taxi stand, with all these Mercedes Benz cars in no specific lines or lanes, and all the drivers shouting something like "Yerushalayim." My first lesson in Hebrew. *Yerushalayim* meant Jerusalem. We packed into a taxi with as many bodies that would fit and headed out to Jerusalem. We found a youth hostel that was full of soldiers coming and going; it was like being back in a barracks, and I just loved it. I met an Australian Jew who was also an IDF Israeli soldier who walked me through the situation and finally suggested I pick up a book called *O Jerusalem* and brush up on the history of the country I was in.

The next day I found a bookstore and bought an English version of the book and began to learn a little bit about the political situation I found myself in. We also went to an agency that placed volunteers in kibbutzim around the country—there was a need everywhere. I, of course, wanted to go where it was the most dangerous. That was easy. We were assigned to a kibbutz in the far north of the country in an area called the Ramata Golan near the Syrian border. The area was still in a firefight, but from what we could gather the Syrian army had been driven back quite a distance from our kibbutz. We boarded a bus and headed north out of Jerusalem, through towns with names like Nazareth and Tiberius, names that took me back to Catholic school in Vancouver, although here they were for real. We passed Lake Tiberius, which I knew as the Sea of Galilee, and started making the long climb up to the Ramata Golan. All along the highway we were being stopped by Israeli soldiers and made to wait as tractor-trailer low beds pulled past us, loaded with Syrian tanks, all of them with a giant Star of David painted over the Syrian emblem. We were told that this was captured equipment, on the way to the southern front to be manned by Israeli tank crews in the fight with the Egyptian army that was still going on. There had been huge losses of tanks and tank crews on both sides in what would later be known as some of the fiercest tank battles since the Battle of the Bulge in Europe in 1944.

When we arrived at our kibbutz the place reminded me of Phu Bai. There were rows of attached houses and some bigger buildings all surrounded by a double chain-link fence with guard towers every couple of hundred meters. Inside the fence were dogs on leads attached to a long wire that allowed them room to run. Everyone I could see was armed with either an M16, an AK-47, or a short, stubby submachine gun I would learn was called an Uzi. I was already familiar with the Uzi, having had one poking into my ribs all the way from Jerusalem. The bus had been so full of armed soldiers that I had to stand all the way, suffering elbows and Uzis.

I noticed that while we were being interviewed by the kibbutz manager, the ground was continually vibrating. The manager said this was coming from a battery of 105's that was continually shelling the other side of the mountain that was between us and the Syrian army. The battery was also on the receiving end of Syrian artillery, but we were out of range of that, at least for the moment.

[34]   Mike Hoover

It was generally thought that I was a Jew from Canada, here to volunteer like a host of others from all over the world. One of the first things I learned was that Jews don't all look alike. There were Americans from New York who looked one way, and there were people from India who looked like Hindus; there were blacks from Chicago and there were blond kids from Australia who looked as though they had just come in from surfing. There were Russians and South Americans, tall redheads, and some people who were short with black hair. I fit right in. It felt like summer camp with guns.

We were crammed into a barracks-like building that had originally served as housing for the first settlers there and now provided *mitnadev* accommodation. It wasn't as bad as Marine Corps barracks but we were plenty crowded. One of the first things I noticed, apart from the obvious military surroundings, was that there were lots of young girls around and if there was one thing I had no experience of it was girls and dating and the like. That would all change and sooner than I ever expected.

The IDF—Israeli Defense Force—regularly sent soldiers with emotional problems to the rear, to stay on the kibbutzim. Some of them had been shaken by too much fighting and just needed a rest while remaining on active duty. Some of them were just plain kooky. That's what I thought when I was swept off my feet by a female officer who was staying on the kibbutz. Everyone ate in a big dining room; mealtimes were the main social events and this is where the first love affair of my life started. When we arrived we were like the flavour of the week and were introduced to what seemed to be hundreds of people. I had never experienced such a friendly atmosphere and this one lady wasn't shy about her intentions. I was too clumsy to take advantage of the situation right away but I must say I was turned on by the mini-skirt and the Uzi hanging over her shoulder. The Israeli female soldiers had the sexiest uniforms, and they would hem up their skirts to make them even more appealing. I had been trained to have the utmost respect for officers and had learned in the corps that never would a lowly private first class become involved with someone from the officer class. It just didn't happen. But here things were different.

I was assigned to work in the fields with about a hundred American kids pulling weeds. These kids were from all the corners of America but mostly from New York City and Chicago where there are large Jewish populations. Most of them spoke a little Hebrew, and that left me in the dark when they spoke to the locals. I became determined to learn to speak the language and started to learn a word a day. Everyone was helpful. The war made everyone pull together and when they saw that this big goy wanted to learn Hebrew they all helped.

One of the jobs that no one wanted was washing the dishes in the dining hall, because you had to get up at four in the morning to do the last evening's dirty dishes. I volunteered and loved it. There were lots of women scurrying around and I would listen carefully to try to pick up a word here and there.

One night when I went to the recreation building one of the American kids asked me if I wanted to play a game of chess. Although the game was popular there, I had never played; however, once I did so my life changed forever. Somehow my mind was designed for chess; when I looked at the board it almost spoke to me. I had to learn the basics, the files, the ranks, and the chessmen but I found I was a natural. I didn't win a game for some time because my opponents were all very experienced players and played with a lot of passion for the game. Eventually I got to winning a few games.

As we acclimatized to life on the kibbutz, the artillery duels continued daily. The ground always vibrated. When my time in the kitchen was up I was assigned to work with some of the men who took care of the cattle, and for this I had to go with some soldiers to take target practice and learn how to field strip the Uzi submachine gun. By now they knew I was a veteran but that didn't mean much to them because everyone there was a veteran and, as the saying went, "everyone in Israel is a frontline soldier." This gave me an opportunity to meet some of the regular army soldiers who were stationed in a little camp outside our wire.

We went to the rifle range and shot off a few rounds and I was taught the workings of the Uzi, the AK-47, and another little 9mm submachine gun called the Carl Gustav. In Vietnam we called it the Swedish K. This was the weapon I was issued. Whenever we went to check on the cattle we had to be armed and in a convoy of at least two jeeps. Whenever we made a stop, the crew from one of the jeeps set up an ambush while the other kibbutznicks went about their chores. It was a lot of extra work but necessary at the time. The cattle were scattered on either side of the border. At times we had to travel through fenced perimeter minefields to get to the cattle grazing on the other side. This was always a little dicey and we were always more alert in these situations. The first time I was sniped at I heard the bullet flutter by my head. It was not very close and was fired from a long way away, but it still would have killed if it had reached its target. That was my baptism of fire, so to speak, and everyone had a good laugh when we got back behind the fence.

I had not been shot at since that day in Quang Tri Province. I must have killed a dozen NVA's that day and it all came back to me that night, in the nightmare of my life. It was a recurring dream but never like this night. The ghosts of men I had killed marched around in my head as though they had been waiting for this moment to show me they would be with me until it was my turn to join them. It was the worst night of my life. I was afraid to go back to sleep, so I got up and wandered around. I was not the only one unable to sleep. I made my way over to the dining hall and joined several young soldiers who had been transferred from regular duty to the kibbutz. When we looked at each other we didn't have to speak a word; we knew we were all being haunted by some unfulfilled ghosts from our different pasts.

The young men told me they were all conscripts, without combat experience, some stationed along the Bar Lev line on the holiest of holy days—Yom Kippur; others were stationed a little farther north of our present position and to the west up near "The Lebanon" on Mount Hermon. One soldier who was stationed in the south told me how they were smoking dope, sun tanning, and sleeping when all hell broke loose. One of the guys said he couldn't even find his rifle. They explained how the Egyptian army began with an artillery barrage and then they sent the infantry across the Suez Canal in rubber rafts. These kids, who had never seen or expected to see actual combat, were in a fight for their lives. They described how they killed hundreds and hundreds of Egyptians until their rifles seized and the machine guns were ready to melt. They fought until they ran out of ammunition and were ordered to pull back and abandon their positions.

Another soldier told quite a different story, the spookiest story I ever heard. Being a combat veteran, I just thought he was suffering some kind of shellshock and kind of humored him. But he insisted what he saw was real.

I knew for a fact that the Israeli army had redeployed hundreds of Syrian tanks, painted a white Star of David on the side, and low-bedded them all the way down to the Sinai Desert to fight the Egyptian army. That I had seen with my own eyes. I presumed that they had just been captured in combat but the more I thought about it something just wasn't right. Hundreds of tanks in good working order without a bullet mark? What happened to their crews? Did they give up their armour corps without a fight? Having been in the military and seen combat I tried but couldn't come up with any plausible reason why an army would abandon that kind of equipment, especially when they had overrun the Israeli positions and nothing stood in the way between their army and Israel.

Here is where it gets spooky. The soldier told me the Syrian tank corps had overrun their positions and were advancing in an orderly fashion south, when he saw the line of tanks stop and, almost in unison, the tank hatches open and soldiers begin climbing out. Entire crews up and out of their vehicles and running for their lives, without a shot being fired. He then told me he turned around and saw, from one end of the horizon to the other, what looked like an ancient army astride camels and horses, armed with spears and bows. There was thousands upon thousands and they appeared to carry up into the clouds. He said he looked from there to the retreating army and couldn't believe his eyes. He shook when he told me this and started crying uncontrollably. I could see there was something here that was beyond comprehension, something prophetic and completely mind boggling.

At once my nightmare seemed trivial. I sat with this soldier for the rest of that evening and he never strayed from his story. We were from totally different cultures, different religions, and different backgrounds but we were both veterans and that was enough to form a bond. He would have preferred to be clubbing in Tel Aviv, anywhere but here.

I made some lifelong friends that night. I also had heard a story that would change my whole system of beliefs, which until now was very simple and uncomplicated. I thought religions, like the operas that I memorized as a child, were all mythical. Whether it was in Italian or Latin or now Hebrew it was all a myth with lots of entertainment value but little truth. I remembered sticking up for the nuns and ending up in the police station. I thought of how when I was knocked unconscious by a "Chi Com" grenade that it was all black until I woke up freezing in an air-conditioned hospital ward. Now a story like this had shaken me to my bones, seeing that soldier and how he couldn't deal with something that stepped beyond the bounds of reality. He was a descendant of the Biblical Israelites, the "Chosen People."

This situation would have fit in quite well four thousand years ago in this place, I thought to myself. I have a bunch of ghosts running around in my brain but this guy has a complete scene out of the Old Testament. We talked the whole night until it was time to go out on patrol. He may have been in a state of shock but now I was also. I had to organize a whole new belief system and I didn't know where to start.

I had never had a girl friend. My few ventures with the opposite sex were with a couple of prostitutes, Mexican and Filipino, and those both ended me up in sick bay, so I was very cautious when this female army officer began to be overly friendly to me. At first I thought I might face a firing squad if I let things get out of hand so I ignored her advances. This only worked for a while. Then one Friday night, "Ariv Shabatt," when they passed around too many bottles of Mogan David, I found myself in her little apartment having sex with a female officer.

She wasn't born in Israel and couldn't claim the name Sabra. She had emigrated with her family from Russia when she was just a baby and had grown up in Netanya where her father was a school teacher and her mother kept their kosher home. She had grown up sneaking away to the beach every chance she got until she was drafted into the army with all her classmates. She had never been away from home and took to army life. As it turned out she became a valuable asset for the IDF and remained in the army after her enlistment time was over. The army was freedom from the strict religious background that she rejected, and her taking up with a "heathen" was part of her rebellion.

It was like summer camp. We both had duties to perform but our meals were always on time. I moved into her apartment. There was no stress, like paying bills or rent. It was really a journey in Utopia like the title of a book that was going around the kibbutz at the time. I enrolled in a school they had on the kibbutz called an "ulpan," which taught a basic Hebrew course. I went to school for half a day and to work for half a day. The language came easily to me, just as chess had. With lots of help from everyone I picked it up fast and was conversing better all the time. The reading and writing was much more difficult.

The ground shaking became almost unnoticeable until we tried to write something in class or tried to take a drink of something in the dining hall but down deep it was taking its toll on me, and my nightmares got worse as the days, weeks, and months wore on.

After a couple of months, Tova and I took a trip down to Jerusalem. Besides seeing the usual sights we spent the better part of a day at the Western Wall of King David's Temple. There was a constant stream of American families gathered together for bar mitzvahs and bat mitzvahs. It reminded me of my confirmation at the Catholic church in Vancouver although when I mentioned it to Tova I could not come up with the meaning or dogma of the Catholic ceremony. The meaning of these ceremonies here were apparent. "No wonder we call you heathens," she said sarcastically. "Is your confirmation a ceremony of the child reaching adulthood?" she asked, and my reply was that I couldn't remember. She was dumbfounded.

We visited the Christian sites and walked along with tour guides as they told the story of the Stations of the Cross. There were not as many tourists as usual because of the war, so it was easy to get close enough to hear the tour guides tell their story. They let us stay with the group in the expectation of receiving a tip. Tova bombarded me with questions about Christianity. She had grown up in a kosher household with strict observances, a strong father figure, and a mother who emphasized tradition. I, on the other hand, grew up learning operas in Italian and religion in Latin, with no understanding of either. She just couldn't get the story of a Jew dying for the heathens then coming back to life after he was put to death by the Romans and then the heathens blaming the Jews for killing him. "Now he's alive. So what's the problem?" she asked.

After some rather stressful days in Jerusalem we boarded a bus to Eilat. The bus was overflowing with both civilians and soldiers, but because Tova was in uniform we were given seats. We traveled south to Be'er Sheba. Here for the first time I actually used some of my Hebrew when I ordered a meal in the bus depot. It was another epiphany for me; up until that time I listened but was afraid to reply, but now for the first time, with her encouragement, I used the language and was understood. It was a fabulous feeling. I could recite entire operas in a foreign language, word for word, without the slightest comprehension. Now, being able to ask for something as simple as a cup of coffee and a falafel made me feel like I belonged.

It is common in Israel to visit other kibbutzim. Tova had some friends living on a kibbutz just north of Eilat so we made that our first destination after Jerusalem. The bus let us off on the side of the highway about forty kilometers north of Eilat, and we walked up a winding road through a canyon into an oasis of beauty. There were date palms surrounding what looked like a resort. There were no double wire fences with savage dogs and guard towers. There were tennis courts and a large swimming pool. There was also a large dairy and melon fields. Tova told me that this was the "Land of Plenty" that Moses had talked about in the Bible.

We were greeted by her friends and they went on and on in Hebrew and I would pick up a word here and there until someone came along and invited me to play tennis. I had never played before but eagerly accepted an offer of lessons. After just a few volleys, my volunteer instructor looked across at me, smiled, and said, "You're a natural; I'll enjoy teaching you." That enthusiastic comment really cheered me up. There must be something in human nature that when just a small compliment is directed your way it makes you feel like a king. Like chess, tennis became part of my kibbutz-learned repertoire.

Tova's friends and now mine also insisted that we travel to Eilat and go for a swim in the Red Sea. They borrowed a vehicle from the kibbutz, and we traveled the forty kilometers to Eilat and my first glimpse of the Red Sea. What a thrill to see the ocean but at the same time to see a resort town completely deserted. The hotels and coffee bars were closed. The only traffic was military vehicles, although there were not many soldiers about. This part of the country had escaped the war. The country of Jordan, along the entire eastern border of Israel, had not joined in the hostilities. The thought in the back of every Israeli's mind was that if Jordan had joined in the war there would have been fighting in the streets of Tel Aviv.

It was the middle of winter, as far as winter goes in the Middle East. It was still very warm and we drove through the deserted city and down to the beach for a swim. Across the water there was what looked like a town and I asked what it was. Tova looked at me the way one would regard an idiot. "Why, that's Aqaba," she exclaimed.

"Aqaba, Aqaba," I repeated over and over again. All I could think of was the movie "Lawrence of Arabia" when Peter O'Toole walked into the officers' club in Cairo all dirty and disheveled and announced, "We've taken Aqaba." I truly had a moment. It never occurred to me that Aqaba was a real place or where it was or anything like that. But there it was. In a land where people talk of thousands of years, Lawrence and his Arab army on camels, crossing the Nefud Desert, storming Aqaba, and capturing the Turkish garrison was like yesterday. In fact, it was only fifty years before, during World War I, when Turkey was the enemy. After reading *O Jerusalem* I realized in World War II the British were the enemy. Then in the 1967 Arab-Israeli War it was all the Arab armies that were the enemy and now, in this war, it was only some of the Arab armies. It was hard to not get confused.

The border runs right down the middle of the gulf, Eilat on one side and Aqaba on the other. One body of water with two names. I thought that must have played hell with the shipping as I watched the giant cargo ships heading both ways, plying the waters up and down the gulf.

The water was cold for December but clear all the way to the bottom. We swam out to a Byzantine ruin on a little island and I was schooled in more history, ancient this time. Around every corner was another history lesson. We found a place to camp for the night and I went to look for some wood for a fire and noticed the strangest thing. Not a branch or a twig; nothing on the beach or surrounding area, no wood to burn. Back in British Columbia you just had to step out of your door to find wood. Again more lessons, this time in geography. We camped out under the stars in this desert with no wood for a fire and no mosquitoes to bother us.

The last time I had camped out at night was in Vietnam and we swatted mosquitoes all night and then picked blood-sucking leeches off our bodies in the morning. The only thing that was similar was that we were just as well armed. In Vietnam we were looking for a fight and would shoot up anything that moved. Here we just wanted to have a good time, not trouble. It was just about as close to heaven as it could get. In the morning we packed up our gear, shook out the sand, and made our way to a little outdoor café in Eilat for some breakfast. We had only been gone from our kibbutz for a couple of days but decided it was time to get back to so we said goodbye to our friends and they dropped us off at the bus depot and with much sadness said goodbye.

The starting point of the bus line was Eilat so it was easy to get a good seat for the trip. The scenery was dry desert until we drove past the Dead Sea and then it was desert and blue water with very little life of any kind. Our first stop was Be'er Sheba, where I got to practice my Hebrew again mustering up enough courage to order coffee and a falafel. The bus then carried us on to Jerusalem. We found a friendly hotel and then went walking in the old city stopping for more falafels and soft drinks, oblivious to everything but ourselves.

CHAPTER FOUR

Tova was determined to find a shop that sold records. She had a little portable phonograph back on the kibbutz and a few old Beatles records that we would listen to over and over again. She wanted to buy a record that was very popular at the time not only in Israel but all over Europe and around the world. It was called "The Dark Side of the Moon" by Pink Floyd. We couldn't find the record in Jerusalem so we caught a taxi into Tel Aviv and wandered down one of the most famous streets in the world, Dizengoff Avenue. There are all kinds of romantic myths surrounding this street with its outdoor cafés and shops. We found a record store and Tova bought her record. We stayed the night in a youth hostel and the next day boarded the bus and began the rest of our journey. I was getting more familiar with the area and seemed to feel at home when the bus stopped at places like Nazareth and Tiberius. After Tiberius we began the long climb up the mountains into the "Ramata Golan" and finally into our little fortress. It was nice to return and be welcomed by the kibbutzniks. I really felt like I belonged.

The days were a set routine. We would gather together very early in the morning, form up in a small convoy, and head out to check on the cattle. Sometimes everyone would meet at one of the huge vegetable fields and we would weed the rows of vegetables all day. My nightmares were off and on and I would meet up with the soldiers in the dining hall on most nights when I couldn't sleep. On one occasion "Avi," the soldier who told me the fantastic story of his biblical vision, told me about Comet Kohoutek. This was a comet that was in the night sky and was going to be at its brightest in a few days. He was convinced that there was something prophetic happening and he wanted to see it for himself. The only problem was that in our little valley the comet was going to be obscured by the huge mountain to the north and east of us. He wanted to climb the mountain late at night and view this celestial phenomenon for himself. After his last vision he was convinced that he was somehow destined to experience something that was unexplainable. The mountain was across the valley in Syrian territory and was considered out of bounds and hostile.

He didn't care and was totally convinced that he had to experience this thing for himself and there was nothing that was going to stop him. He told me that there were only a few days left before the comet would be at its brightest and he was going to slip away from the kibbutz at night and walk up the mountain. He asked me if I wanted to come along. If I wasn't going through my own hell at night I might have shrugged it off, but being a highly trained recon marine I was easily talked into the lark.

There would be many obstacles in our way, the first one being perhaps the hardest: getting out of our fortress at night. The main gate would be shut and locked. The dogs would all be on their chains and the guard towers would be manned. Any movement would bring a response from the garrison that was located outside our fence and down the main highway a short distance. We had a few days to plan our adventure and my accomplice "Avi" and I were getting more determined as we made our plans.

There were Israeli folk songs about crazy larks by soldiers who would sneak over the Jordanian border and visit the old Roman city of Petra and bring back some souvenir to show off. In reality some of the adventurers who had tried it had gotten themselves killed when trying to live out the words of the folk songs.

I was totally convinced by this point that we were going to accomplish something providential and become some kind of mythical heroes. Who said that "youth was wasted on the young?"

Avi and I met every night for a week. We finally agreed that the only way to get past our first obstacle was for him to volunteer for guard duty at the military post. During the daylight hours we decided it would be easy for me to mingle with the soldiers on duty as I already knew quite a few of them, considering that we all ate together in the kibbutz dining hall. Also by now I had been out on many patrols with the IDF regulars stationed there. They were assigned to accompany us with their jeeps and flatbed trucks with the mounted .50 caliber machine guns. Most of the regulars at the post were draftees and younger than me but there was a good contingent of reservists who were older and much more experienced. Avi was a regular but on a light duty posting because of the tremendous losses his outfit had suffered in the first days of the war.

Our plan was for Avi to volunteer but at the last moment, once we were in the barracks, Avi would come down with an illness and have to be replaced by another soldier. We couldn't have him volunteer and then go AWOL; if he got caught he could face a firing squad—and me too, for that matter.

Sneaking out of the army post would be a lot easier. They didn't have a perimeter fence, just bunkers with lots of armour. Gathering the necessary equipment would be easy also as there was an armoury on the post with lots of weapons of every type. There were also lots of old used uniforms lying around that would be necessary if we were spotted by friendly troops.

I told Tova about our plan and she threatened to turn us in. She said we were crazy and we would get ourselves killed. At that point I wished I had kept my mouth shut, but for Avi there was no turning back and I was compelled to go along even though it was as she described—beyond crazy.

The next day I met Avi in the dining hall at lunch time and he informed me it was all set. He would meet me after work and while the gates were still open we would walk down the road to the army camp and mingle with the soldiers. We met up that afternoon and strolled out the front gates like nothing was happening and walked right into the army camp together. He was in uniform and armed and I looked just like a kibbutznick, nothing out of the ordinary.

I found a uniform that fit me and a pack. I had learned what the most important equipment was back in my marine recon days and knowing we might be out for a couple of days I kept that in mind. The most important was, of course, ammunition. We wouldn't have a radio so there would be no support if we got into trouble. Some of the equipment was standard American issue like the hand grenades, M16 rifles, and ammo. We both chose the smaller, lighter Uzi submachine gun with lots of ammo and eight hand grenades each. There was no Special Forces type dried food so we picked up some fruit and bread and crackers. Water would be very important so we both packed six canteens. Our packs were not light but at the same time they weren't the eighty-pound packs I had humped when I was a line grunt. Avi also found a starlight scope and packed it up with his gear. It would be our eyes when we had to find a way to pass through the Syrian lines.

When darkness fell we painted our faces black and slipped out of the compound unnoticed on our providential mission.

At first we walked right down the center of the highway. Then we moved off the road, having to negotiate around the Israeli minefields. I had already been made aware of where the openings were in the fence. We would drive our jeeps through these places on our patrols during the day. As for the other side, there was no fence and no minefields that we were aware of, but we would have to move slowly until we were past their first outposts. Once through the hole in the fence we traveled fast across the no man's land that separated the two countries. It wasn't hard to find the first outpost because you could hear music in the distance. We found it easy to creep up on them just close enough to mark their position in our minds and move past them heading toward out objective. When we were close enough to make out their music I couldn't believe my ears. I expected to hear Arab music, the kind I heard all over the old city of Jerusalem, but to my dismay it was Pink Floyd's "The Dark Side of The Moon."

"Holy shit," I said under my breath. Here we were two opposing military forces hell bent on wiping each other out and both listening to the same tunes. Something just didn't make sense.

We stopped while Avi scanned the area with the starlight scope and then we slipped past the listening post to where the mountain began to rise out of the valley. We knew it would take time to reach the bottom of the mountain but it took longer then we expected, so with our first obstacle behind us and the first signs of daylight beginning to show we decided to find some cover and lay up and get our bearings. We began to climb out of the valley when birds started singing and we knew we had to find cover fast so as not to disturb their daily pattern. Any astute soldiers who were expecting to hear singing birds at daybreak and didn't hear the sounds starting to carry across the valley would become suspicious and send out a patrol, and that could be the end of us.

We found an outcropping of rocks that would provide us some cover and hunkered down. We had traveled a short distance up the mountain with the all the tough climbing ahead of us. The dawn was now breaking and as we got a better picture of where we were, we could see the sand-bagged observation post we had avoided and another one about a hundred meters to the north. We looked for another to the south of us but we guessed because of ground rising the next bunker must be farther up the mountain. We then decided to get some sleep, so we curled up back to back and took our Uzis off safety.

I woke up a couple hours later to the smell of food. The soldiers below us had started a fire and were cooking their breakfast. The smoke wafted up to our position and past. It was full light now and there was no sound of the birds. I crawled out from behind our hiding spot and raised my head up very slowly to see what it looked like in the light of day. There was a lot of movement below us, and from our height advantage I could see that our cover should keep us a secret as long as no patrols were sent our way. We would, however, have to remain here until nightfall as there was no way we could move out with all the action below us.

We presumed there would be lookouts up the side of the mountain and probably an artillery position right on the top. In our exuberance to witness this comet there were some important factors we had failed to take into account and now we would have to deal with them. We knew it would be risky before we started out, and now we were convinced it would be fatal if we were discovered.

We stayed at our position all day. Most of the movement below only happened at mealtimes and as soldiers in every army find out, there is a lot of stand-down time and the proverbial "hurry up and wait." As night fell we plotted our ascent up the face of the mountain, ate some bread, and then moved out. We now knew we had embarked on this adventure with limited intelligence; the mountain was going to be a harder climb than expected. We were young and in excellent condition, half crazy, and now more determined than ever.

With the help of the starlight scope we would climb a few meters on all fours then get our bearing and continue on. The going was slow and we climbed all night. Every time we stopped to plot our coordinates, it seemed we weren't making much progress. After about eight hours of climbing, the birds started rustling again and we knew we would have to find a place to hide for the day. We never mentioned it but I knew by now we would be missed back on the other side of the border, and with the excellent Druse trackers that patrolled the fence everyone would know where we had gone.

We finally stopped when day began to break and we could see all the way to Mount Hermon and into southern Lebanon. We couldn't tell how much farther we had to climb because of the steepness. We were, however, in a much better position to go unnoticed. Our rest was short-lived when we noticed how cold it had become; our exertion had kept our body temperature up and our hot sweat soon turned cold and we began to shiver. We had failed to take this into consideration in our planning and we only packed light blankets so we bundled up as best we could back to back and fell asleep.

We slept for a few hours until the cold became intolerable so we got up and shook the cobwebs out. We then reconnoitered the ridge above us and saw the snow. We talked about abandoning our quest but after psyching ourselves up we decided we were close enough to make it and we should carry on. We sat and shivered the rest of the day covered up in our light blankets. I used the time to practice my Hebrew with Avi correcting my grammar. We began telling stories of our youth and what it was like growing up on opposite sides of the world. Avi was startled to find out I wasn't a Jew. He just took it for granted, it didn't matter to him—he just found it highly unusual. He said I was the first "goy" he had ever met and wondered if all "goys" were as crazy as me.

When night fell we checked our position and headed up toward our final destination. There was still a lot of mountain to cover and now we would be leaving tracks so we decided when we reached a position where we could see the comet that we would take some pictures, spend a little time to see if we would experience an epiphany, and then head home. The climb began to warm us up and soon the steepness became a gradual drop until the ground began to level out. We stopped to check out the terrain with the starlight scope, thinking this would be a good place for a lookout position. We hoped that if there were soldiers on the top of this mountain they would be asleep or huddled around a warm stove. We didn't think anyone would ever expect an enemy patrol to be this far north and certainly not climbing up this rock face. If ever there would be a commando raid this far north they would be inserted by helicopter and then everyone would know what was going on.

We walked on until we found a position where we could see and photograph the comet and there it was, Comet Kohoutek. The ball of light was easy to distinguish among all the stars with its bright tail trailing behind. It wasn't as bright as we expected and we weren't experiencing anything mystical, at least I wasn't, but it was still a wonderful feeling of accomplishment. The main thing I noticed was the cold. Our location was covered in a wet snow and we were becoming soaked through to our skin. Avi said he doubted that the little camera that he brought along would actually show the comet as it wasn't really all that bright. He said we had to bring back some other kind of trophy to prove we had actually made the trek up this mountain. He said the soldiers that had been to Petra and were held up as folk heroes had all brought back something to prove they had completed their mission.

We decided we would find something on the way back; we just didn't know what. Our decent down the mountain was going to be much faster than the way up because we now knew the terrain and where the lookout posts were located. We made very good time down the mountain but were force to lay up again in our first hiding place as dawn began to break and the birds started to sing. We were cold, wet, hungry, and thirsty but we were out of the snow. We hunkered down covered up as best we could and went to sleep. Again the routine of the Syrian soldiers woke us up with the smell of the fire smoke and breakfast cooking. Our stomachs growled as we fidgeted back to back trying to put the noise and smells out of our minds. We managed to sleep most of the day back to back, and covered up by our blankets we managed to produce enough heat to make it tolerable. Avi kept saying we needed a trophy otherwise the entire adventure would be wasted and I was at a loss as to what we could do.

When night finally fell and we packed up to move out we could hear the music again coming from the first listening post we had skirted around. Avi looked at me and said, "We are going to get that record."

"What do mean?" I said. "There must be three or four soldiers in that hootch. What are we going to do about them?"

"No problem," said Avi and he unsheathed his knife and rubbed it across his sleeve. "I'm not going back without that record."

"Holy shit!" I said. "You're fuckin' crazy."

"I would rather die here than go back without a trophy," Avi stated emphatically.

I kind of understood what he was saying. I remembered when I was a line grunt there were a few guys in my platoon who collected ears of dead NVA. After a while they began to smell but it wasn't until the captain came by and gave the guys hell that they actually got rid of the rotting ears. I guess those guys didn't mind the smell. I just know I wasn't in a position to say anything at the time or my own ears might have ended up around their necks.

I asked Avi what the plan was. We were still a couple hundred meters from their position and the music carried loud and clear on the still night. He said he would have to get close enough to see how many soldiers there were in the bunker and with the noise he indicated it would be easy. He told me to sit tight, he would reconnoiter their position, and then come back and we would make a plan.

We made our way to within fifty meters and then Avi left me in the rocks and crept toward the music. He was gone at least an hour before he returned, telling me he was able to move right up to the gun opening and look in. He said that they had an oil lamp for light and there were three of them in there. He also said the music was not coming from a record player; it was a cassette player and it was located at the back of the bunker.

Avi, like many Israelis, spoke fluent, impeccable Arabic and his plan was to sneak up to their opening, pretend he was an officer, and call the soldiers out of their bunker. We would then find something to tie them up with and make off with the cassette. If that didn't work we would kill them all. Either way we weren't going home empty-handed.

We waited at our position, shivering in the cold, until late in the night. We debated back and forth and decided if we found them asleep Avi would sneak in and steal the tape without disturbing them and then we could be on our way. There was still a faint light coming out of the gun slits from their coal oil lamp when we started the crawl toward the bunker.

When we finally got close enough to look through the opening we could see the three soldiers bundled up and apparently asleep. Avi unsheathed his bayonet and signaled me to do the same. We had to be ready if they woke up. We then crawled around to their door opening and Avi went in first. I was right behind him keeping my eyes on the sleeping soldiers. Avi crept on his tiptoes, negotiating around the cluttered space as best he could when he inadvertently stepped on one of the soldier's feet and startled him awake. The soldier leapt up, uncovering himself from his blanket, and without any hesitation Avi sunk his bayonet into the soldier's chest. When the next one awoke I did the same, only I came across Avi's back with an upward stroke and plunged my knife upwards under the man's jaw, forcing the blade all the way into his skull. While I was doing this Avi dispatched the third soldier before he could even rise up. In a matter of a few seconds they were all dead. When I thrust my blade into my victim his warm blood gushed out, covering my face and chest and impairing my vision for a moment. My blade was stuck in the man's skull, so with my left hand I had to hold onto my victim and retrieve my knife with the other. While I wiped the blood from my eyes Avi reached for the cassette player, popped it open, grabbed the cassette, and turned for the door.

I was right behind him. We didn't waste any time in our retreat. My heart was pounding out of my chest. I had just killed a man with a knife; I had never done that before. In my training at boot camp, Staff Sergeant Mejia had made me challenge him with a knife on several occasions but he had always disarmed me with ease before leaving me in a heap on the ground. I had always wondered if I would be able to make a kill if I was faced with the situation and now I had my answer.

We hurried back to where we had left our packs, stopped for a few seconds to listen to see if we had been discovered, and then began our journey home, running as fast as we could. The blood was starting to coagulate on my uniform and as it was cooling down it become sticky. As we began to heat up from our forced march my sweat began to mix with the blood and the smell began to make me nauseous. There would be no stopping now, and as the dawn began to break and the birds started up we increased our pace. There was now at least a mile of open country ahead of us to traverse and we would be out in the open very soon. Our packs now became our worst enemy. Our canteens were empty but we still had all our ammo and the hand grenades that might become handy if we were intercepted. We knew when the dead soldiers were discovered that vehicular patrols would be sent out to find us before we got back to the border and they would be shooting at anything that moved.

We were almost out in the open when we heard the jeep coming up behind us, its engine roaring but still out of sight. The headlights were the first indication that the jeep was headed our way and there was no way we could outrun it so we hunkered down in a dip in the terrain and prepared an ambush. I opened my pack and lined up my hand grenades and my Uzi. I put the indicator on full auto, laid the weapon on the ground in front of me, and then I pulled the pins on two grenades. I would have to time it perfectly. When I figured the jeep was four seconds away I began hurling the grenades in its path. I had time to throw four of them before the jeep drove up and in tandem they exploded. Avi then sprayed the vehicle with his Uzi and I picked up my weapon and did the same. We caught them by complete surprise. The vehicle burst into flames and ran off the track. We didn't wait around; we just picked up our gear and began running for our lives.

We traveled a couple hundred meters before we heard the sound of the second vehicle. This one didn't have the same roaring sound but they had obviously found the first wreck, attended to their dead and dying, and thought it best to proceed with caution. For all they knew we could be a commando recon unit with air support and with greater numbers than just two.

All of this commotion had alerted the people on the other side of the border who were already out searching for us. We had been missing for three days and nights and had been tracked as far as the border. After that it was a total mystery as to our whereabouts.

We kept up as fast a pace as we could when .50 caliber tracers began shooting over our heads. We immediately hit the ground. If they found our range we would be torn to bits. When we looked back we couldn't see where the firing was coming from so we assumed it was only a probe, random firing. Our little 9mm submachine guns were useless at this range and we knew we would have to either wait for them and try to spring another ambush or get picked off as they raked the ground with their armour-piercing rounds.

Some people don't believe in miracles. We on the other hand happened to be on this adventure because Avi claimed he had witnessed a miracle. I for my part had been convinced that Avi was telling the truth because I had witnessed all the Syrian tanks being transported south with the Star of David painted over the Syrian emblem. Then there was the comet. And now we were both facing almost certain death with the .50 calibers opening up on us with short, probing bursts. We looked each other in the eye knowing there would be no way out of this one but for a miracle—then we heard the thumping rotors of a helicopter gunship and the firing of anti-tank missiles along with the steady staccato of machine gun fire.

The cavalry had arrived! We got up running and as we used to say in Vietnam we "beat feet out of there." As the missiles crashed into the Syrian armour and the machine gun fire rained down on them we never stopped until we were through the fence and on the other side of the border.

Waiting for us were at least a platoon of reservists, not to mention several tanks on low beds and jeeps with mounted machine guns. Everyone was wondering who we were and what in the hell we were doing on the other side of the fence. This theatre of operation had been relatively quiet and the big artillery duels that were happening were farther north and there had been no recent incursions on either side of the border in this area. We were desperate for water and grabbed the first canteens that were offered to us. Then there was a frenzy of questions, all in Hebrew, and I didn't understand a word.

We looked a mess. Dried blood covered both of us and we were wild-eyed, reduced to our primeval core. We were both ushered to a medical tent and given physicals. When that was complete and we were partially cleaned up, we were taken to another tent. Sitting in this tent were several Israeli officers who showed no emotion. One of them, the junior of the three, indicated for us to sit down. These were some of the only words I understood. The debriefing was all in Hebrew. I could sort of get the gist of what was going on with Avi doing all the talking and when I was asked a question I just grunted and played dumb. Being completely outfitted in Israeli military gear from the uniform to the boots they at first wanted to know my unit until Avi explained I was a "mitnadev" from the kibbutz and not in the army. This they already knew as we had both been reported missing. Avi then produced the cassette tape covered with dried blood as his trophy. They were unbelievably calm; they were seasoned soldiers from several wars who didn't seem impressed at all by the story.

They then started to question me in perfect English. They went on to explain that they were officers assigned to a special unit called the "Sharav Unit." This unit was mostly composed of psychologists and psychiatrists along with Special Forces. They explained how at times in Israel when the atmospheric conditions were right the country was bombarded with positive ions, and it made some people go crazy. It happened more often to Christian pilgrims on trips to Sinai and in the southern deserts where there had been numerous dried-out bodies found in the Negev and Ariva. Some people were turned overly violent and that was how they were going explain this situation. It is commonly known as "the Sharav wind" and everyone had apparently heard of it but us.

They were interested in my military experience and treated me like a soldier and one of their own. They were quite understanding, but it was obvious they knew Avi was posted to the kibbutz because he was suffering from shellshock and they blamed him for taking me on this crazy adventure. Then they said that if the two countries were not in a state of war we would have been charged with murder. They also let us know matter-of-factly that if any of their soldiers had been injured there would have been a very different outcome, indicating long prison sentences in a military brig, and it didn't matter if I was in the IDF or not. As it turned out, they had a military category for this sort of thing and buried the situation at the bottom of a pile of paperwork.

CHAPTE SIX

Avi and I were welcomed back to the kibbutz by the manager. We were hungry and tired and still had our blood-soaked uniforms on. He told us that this kind of insanity would not be tolerated, and for me in particular he expected I would be deported when the full extent of the situation was realized by the government officials. We were told we weren't allowed to carry firearms unless we were under attack and if I was to remain I was to report back in the dining hall to do the dishes.

The dishwashing job was on the bottom of the list as far as the volunteers were concerned but I was prepared to do anything as long as they allowed me to stay. It was late in the morning when I finally made my way to Tova's apartment. As I came to the door I could hear from the outside music coming from her portable record player. It was Pink Floyd's "Dark Side of the Moon." I stopped dead in my tracks outside her door. I began shaking like a leaf as the previous three days began to unfold in my mind. The music droned on through the open window and I fell to my knees and covered my head and burst into tears. Tova was inside and didn't know I had returned. After a few minutes I was able to compose myself and I sheepishly knocked on the door. When she answered it she went crazy with joy and we fell into each others arms. She just kept saying "You're alive, you're alive," and burst into tears.

It wasn't long before she noticed the smell and backed off. "You need a shower," she said and led me into the little apartment, stripped the stinky, blood-caked clothes off of me, and pushed me into the bathroom. "Don't come out until you have gotten rid of that stink," she said while gathering up my pile of clothes and heading out the door. I climbed into the shower and turned on the hot water. I had dried blood in my hair and ears along with three days of body grime. We had been given a bit of a cleaning in the medical tent but the real dirt needed a lot of scrubbing to be removed. When I finished my shower and dried off I just had time to crawl into bed before I fell into a deep sleep.

The next thing I remember was the kibbutz manger kicking the side of the bed and yelling at me, "We are not children, get up!" It was 0:400 and time to get down to the kitchen and do the previous night's dishes. The system was that the last night's dishes were washed the first thing in the morning and that was my new duty. I had done dishes before so I didn't need any training. I was up and out of bed "on the double" and ran all the way to the dining room. I was half starved and started picking the last night's leftovers off the dishes, still acting like the wild animal I had resembled over the previous three days. By the time the people started filing in for their breakfast I could tell they were all talking about me, some pissed off at me for disrupting their schedules and making them go out on search parties and others who winked and smiled and slapped me on the back for being a hero. In a place where bravery is not only common but expected I made a pretty good impression for a "goy."

I was kind of feeling full of myself when the kibbutz manager took me aside and told me this thing was not over yet, that they had monitored the Syrian radio communications and eleven soldiers had been killed and several wounded. "If they transfer some of their artillery to the mountain you climbed, this could become a new front and it could cost many more lives and probably not just enemy ones," he said. The IDF had already transferred Avi to a medical facility south of Tel Aviv for evaluation and they were waiting for a decision from the government as to what to do with me. He said he was going to strongly recommend that I be deported back to Canada and let them deal with me.

I was never late again. I made sure I was early on the job and at night when Tova wasn't tutoring me in Hebrew I would go to the recreation hall and play chess. I was getting better with both every day for someone with only an eighth-grade education. My constant memorizing of operas in a foreign language must have helped. Tova likened it to training a dog.

After about a month I was called into the kibbutz manager's office. I felt this must be it. I was going to get the boot and I was beginning to think of how I was going to handle it. When I walked into his office there was a man and a woman sitting there and they looked me over like I was lunch. I was asked to be seated and after they were introduced, the manager got up and excused himself. The man and the woman told me the name of their government department and then they started asking me questions. They would ask a question and then both would take notes as I answered. The questions were all written down in front of them and they started from my childhood until the present. My military experience was of particular interest to them. Some of the questions led me to believe that they had my military file right in front of them. I had to go over the story about how I originally came to be in their country, how, when I was going to college on the GI Bill and was so moved by Golda Meir's speech I dropped everything and boarded the bus to New York City.

The interview lasted for over four hours with no breaks. I could tell the interviewers were Sabras from their accents but couldn't figure out where this could be leading.

They finally began to question me about Avi and his biblical vision and then our adventure across the border. The questioning got very intense when I got to the part where we had killed the three soldiers with our bayonets. They made me play out this part over and over again. They wanted to know my exact feelings. And then the female official asked me point blank if I could do it again.

Up until this point I felt they were some kind of police either charging me with murder or immigration officials getting the paperwork in order to deport me, but that question told me they had something else in mind. They also wanted to know how I felt about the political situation, about which I hadn't a clue. I told them I had read *O Jerusalem* and seen the movie "Exodus" but apart from that I had no idea what was going on. I even went on to tell them I couldn't find this place on a map before I came here. I was exhausted when the interview ended. They matter-of-factly dismissed me and said they would be in touch.

I went back to my daily routine of washing the dishes, struggling through listening to Tova's portable record player, studying Hebrew, and playing chess. The days turned into weeks and then one day when I was in the kitchen doing my job Tova came in and informed me she had been transferred and was to report to an army base in the Sinai Desert and would be gone within a week. We were both devastated. I wouldn't even be able to visit. It was just the way things were and we had to accept it. We spent the next week making all kinds of plans but in our hearts we knew we might never see each other again. Then one morning she boarded the bus and was gone.

I was lost and heartbroken and was thinking of going back to Canada when that very day I was called into the manager's office again, and sitting there were the two government officials. It seemed a little fishy to me but I sat down and waited for what I thought was the bad news. I didn't care at this point and was ready to leave the country.

The female official got right to the point. She wanted to know exactly how, with me being a Canadian, I had come to join the U.S. military. She asked me if I knew what a psychopath was and if I thought I might be one. Being a high school dropout I had no answers for her, only that I had joined the marines for no other reason than what the billboards said. And when she asked if I enjoyed killing, I was truly aghast. I explained I was having recurring nightmares and was very uneasy about my role in what had happened. She then asked me if I would consider joining a secret elite organization that sometimes had to take out enemies of the state of Israel. I was shocked and speechless. I had been waiting to be given my notice to leave the country or even arrested, but here they were offering me a job. "Why me?" I asked. "I don't speak your language yet and I'm not even a Jew."

She wouldn't elaborate; she just said, "If you are interested you will be sent to Tel Aviv for training. We'll give you one week to think about it," adding before I was dismissed that I was to keep this conversation to myself. If they heard that I mentioned this to anyone the offer would be rescinded and I would be deported immediately. I left the office in a daze and went back to my dishes.

There was never really anything to consider; stay here and end up being kitchen help or go on one more adventure. Tova was gone and it seemed this was part of the plan. Avi was in a nuthouse and I could see no reason to stay on the kibbutz any longer.

It didn't take more than a minute to organize my backpack when they showed up a week later. The female official had my passport in her hand when they came to gather me up. There was no send off. Everyone on the kibbutz was going about his business when we climbed into the car and drove out of the gates and headed south. I was in the back seat and the two officials in the front and they were paying a lot of attention to my passport. Speaking only in Hebrew and not allowing me into the conversation I thought it a little weird and got a little paranoid. I began to think this was all just a ruse and that they were really just taking me to the airport to put me on a plane back to Canada.

CHAPTE SEVEN

We drove straight through to Tel Aviv. I had no idea where we were when we pulled up to a double gate with armed guards. We drove through the gates and into a very large compound. The male official told me to leave my backpack and get out of the car and follow him. When we got out of the car we were joined by two armed guards, one on either side of me, and escorted into a building. Once in the building I was marched down a long corridor, down several flights of stairs, and into a room. The door was closed behind me and locked. The room contained a single cot, a desk, a sink, and a toilet. I was in a prison cell.

I was too tired to get upset and fell onto the bed and went to sleep. The next thing I heard was the rattle of a key chain and then a key entering the door lock, the tumblers turning, and then the door opening. I looked up from my cot to see what was happening. The door opened a crack and a plate of food was pushed in and across the floor, then the door closed. I then realized I was starving. I hadn't eaten all day. I got up and went over to pick up the tray and placed it on the desk and proceeded to eat.

I began to think that I was in prison and everything they
had told me was a lie. I was being charged with murder and I
might spend the rest of my life in this cell. I began to panic.
After I finished eating I began to pace the cell. I counted
out the number of steps from one end to the other. There
was no window and there was no light switch. I still had my
watch and was carefully keeping an eye on the time when at
precisely 20:00 hours the lights went out. The only light left
was coming from under the door, and once my eyes adjusted
I could make out the shadow of the bed and the desk. I didn't
bother to undress. I lay on the bed and tried to fall asleep.
Then I crawled under the covers but couldn't sleep for hours.
The whole situation continued to play itself out in my mind.
What had I got myself into and how was I going to get myself
out? No one knew I was here. I didn't even know where here
was.

The next morning I was awakened by the rattling of the
keys and then the lights turning on. I looked at my watch
and it was 0:400. Then came the sound of the keys entering
the door lock, the tumblers turning, and the door opening.
I could see the same two guards standing at the open door,
one holding a tray of food and the other holding an Uzi. The
first guard placed the breakfast tray on the floor and told me
in Hebrew to hand him the empty tray. He then backed up
and closed the door. The next sound was the key turning in
the lock and then silence. I picked up the tray, placed it on
the desk, and then proceeded to the sink and splashed some
water on my face. There was one little towel on a rack and
I used it to dry my face. I sat down at the desk and ate the
food they had brought me. The food included a cup of coffee
that was cold but I drank it anyway. It tasted just fine. I ate
everything on the tray and it still wasn't enough.

At 0:800 I could hear the sound of footsteps coming down
the corridor and the rattle of keys. I was becoming used to
the routine—the rattle of the keys, the key being inserted in
the lock, the tumblers turning, and the door opening. It was

the same two guards. One of the guards instructed me to bring the tray and then he motioned me to follow him. Once out of the cell the guard with the Uzi fell in behind me while I followed the other guard. When we passed by a food cart he told me to place the tray down on the cart and keep moving. I could see several other empty trays on the cart, indicating to me that I was not alone in this place. As we marched down the corridor I noticed there was a door on each side about every ten feet. "I am in a prison," I thought to myself as we marched along the corridor and up the stairs.

We eventually came to the first door that I had entered the day before and then proceeded out into the open-air compound. When we had arrived the day before it was in the late afternoon and the place was almost empty, but now it was much different. People in uniforms and people in civvies were moving in every direction. They were all traveling in double time and no one stopped to look at me or my escorts. I was led across the compound to another building and ushered in the door and down another long corridor. We eventually came to a door and the guard in the lead signaled me to halt. He then made me turn to the side and place my nose against the wall. He whispered in Hebrew in my ear not to move, which I understood perfectly. He then proceeded to knock on the door and enter, closing it behind him. The other guard stood silently beside me never taking his eyes off of me.

The door opened and the guard called out to me in Hebrew to enter the room. As I passed through the door the smell of cigarette smoke caught my senses. I entered into what looked like an office. Sitting at a desk was one man in a military uniform without any insignia. I couldn't tell what rank he might have been and judging from his age I guessed he must have been a high-ranking officer. There was a chair in front of his desk and he motioned me to sit down, while he puffed on his "Time" cigarette and read a file on the desk in front of him.

Without looking up he spoke to me in English in a strong Sabra accent. He asked me if I knew why I was here. I replied that it looked like I was in prison and that it was probably because of my adventure with Avi. He kept reading and puffing and without looking up he asked me where my loyalties lay. My mind went back to my first encounter with the Vancouver police in Sister Superior's office when I was just a boy. They also had asked me questions that I hadn't any answer for. I explained that when I was in the corps my loyalty was first to my squad, then the platoon, and then the marines and then to the USA.

"You are not an American," he said, "and you fought and probably killed men under a foreign flag. And then you caused the deaths of eleven Syrian soldiers; one you apparently killed with a knife." I was beginning to panic. He butted out his cigarette and lit another; he didn't offer me one and I didn't ask. He then looked up from his desk for the first time. I had seen that look before. It took me back to my first day as a line grunt when one of the men on my rifle team threatened to kill me if I fucked up. It was the look of a killer. There is no other look like it in the world. It is in the eyes and I guess it was in mine. In Vietnam we called it the ten-thousand-yard stare but that was just a euphemism for killer's eyes. His stare seemed to penetrate right through me.

His eyes went back to the file in front of him and he began to ask me questions about my childhood, sometimes looking at me while at other times his eyes would never leave the page. When something seemed to interest him he would write it down. He asked me about my brothers and sisters and what it was like growing up in Canada. He had a way to bring things out of me that I hadn't thought of for years. I thought to myself that I had gone over all of this back at the kibbutz and where could it be leading? We went over and over the part when I had been a child and had thought I was defending the faith only to be punished for my actions. He was also very interested to know why I was so moved by Golda's speech that I dropped everything and flew off to uncertainty in this country. This went on for a couple hours and then he looked at his watch and abruptly closed the file and said we would continue this tomorrow.

He must have pushed a button or the guards were listening in because immediately the door opened and one of the guards entered and called out to me in Hebrew to come with him. I stood up from my chair and followed the guard out of the door and down the corridor, one guard in front and one behind the same way we came in. We left the building from the same door, walked across the compound and into the building where I had spent the previous night. We followed the same procedure as the day before but when they opened the door to my cell a jumpsuit and a towel were lying on my cot. I was instructed to pick them up, and we walked farther down the corridor to a washroom with showers where I stripped off my kibbutz clothes and showered. The guards never left me alone for a second, there was no door or shower curtain, and I showered with them in full view and toweled off, left my clothes in a heap on the floor, climbed into the jumpsuit, and was escorted back to my cell. On the way back there was a food tray sitting on a cart and I was instructed to pick it up and to continue on.

Once back in the cell I heard the now familiar sound of the door closing behind me, the key in the lock, the tumblers turning, and then the silence. I placed the tray on the desk and began to ponder my situation. I had not bothered to ask anyone if I was allowed to leave or if I was in fact a prisoner. I ate my meal in silence thinking of boot camp back in California when I was broken down by the drill sergeants and then built back up again and I was thinking this treatment was similar in one way but very different in another. In boot camp, no one ever showed any interest in who you were. We were taught to follow orders implicitly. Here they seemed to be breaking me down in another way.

When I finished my meal I wasn't tired but I lay down on my cot anyway. As I looked up at the ceiling I noticed the ceiling tiles had a pattern and it reminded me of a chessboard. I counted out eight vertical rows and eight horizontal. There was no difference in the color so I had to repeat counting over and over again. In my mind I drew a square and then I placed the imaginary square on the ceiling. I then created the files, the vertical rows of squares. The ceiling tiles had holes in them so I chose four for each file. I went back and forth across the square until I could imagine eight vertical rows. Then I concentrated on the ranks, the horizontal rows. I again chose four holes and counted out eight. I then had my chessboard but the effort had put me to sleep.

I woke up to hear the now familiar rattle of keys, the key inserted in the door, and the turning of the tumblers. The door opened and the guard was holding another tray of food. It was time for dinner. He signaled for me to hand him the empty tray. We exchanged trays and he was out the door, locking it behind him. I didn't know the time because I had left my watch in the shower room but in my mind I decided it was 18:00 hours. This time on the tray along with the food was a small toothbrush and a small tube of toothpaste and I used them before I ate my meal. It felt good to clean my teeth.

I finished my meal and decided to do some exercises. I took the chair from the desk and placed my feet on it with my hands on the ground and started doing push-ups. I stopped at fifty feeling the pain in my chest and arms but quite satisfied at the number. I then did the same number of sit-ups and having not done any for quite a while I had to stop at forty. Then with nothing else to do I was back on my cot creating my chessboard. I had to start at the beginning with the squares, first the ranks and then the files and then I tried the diagonals. This is where it got complicated and everything got fuzzy. My brain crashed and I had to stop. I finally fell asleep before lights out and woke up to the sound of the rattle of keys.

The routine was getting old after only two days and today I intended to ask if I was free to leave or if I was a prisoner. The guard entered, we exchanged trays in silence the same as before, and he was gone. I decided it was 0:400 hours and I would start my day. After I brushed my teeth with some delight, I ate breakfast. My chest, stomach, and arms hurt because of the push-ups and sit-ups but I drove myself to go through the drill again. First the fifty push-ups; the pain was not unbearable but it was certainly apparent. And then the sit-ups, and again the pain was there to be dealt with in the same manner. Then it was back to the cot and my chessboard.

The third day, and I was beginning to get into a routine. Again the ranks and then the files and then the hard part, the diagonals. It was all I could do. I went over it and over it. First with my eyes open and then closed. When I closed my eyes it would take a few seconds but then there they would be. I was learning how to concentrate by repetition.

I presumed it was 0:800 when the door was unlocked and I was ordered to follow the guards again, one in front and the other trailing behind with his Uzi. Down the corridor past the other doors that I presumed were cells also. Then it came to me. I wondered, are these other cells empty or occupied? I held that thought as we crossed the compound and into the other building. The action in their courtyard or parade ground was the same as the previous day and, as before, no one seemed to notice I even existed. We entered the building through the same door and marched on down the hall, and again I was instructed to place my nose against the wall in the same manner as the day before while the one guard knocked on the door and entered. He returned immediately and motioned me into the room.

The same officer was sitting at his desk and he was smoking the same kind of cigarette. Without looking up he told me in Hebrew to sit, which I understood.

Before we got underway I got up the courage and asked him if I was a prisoner and was I allowed to leave. He looked up from his reading and then held up my passport and my return plane ticket to New York and told me I was free to leave that very moment. He said that at my request he would arrange for a ride to the airport that very morning. He then shook my return ticket to New York and said, "What will it be?" I didn't hesitate. I told him I was staying.

This morning he made me go through every memory I had of my adventure with Avi, everything I could remember. He especially wanted me to go over the part when I killed the Syrian soldier with the bayonet. He then listened carefully to me explain how we had escaped our pursuers after we had been discovered. I didn't hesitate to confirm the fact that unless the helicopter gunships had been on the scene we would never have survived. I could tell he was testing how I reacted under extreme pressure. He then asked me, "Why do you think my organization might be interested in you?"

I said, "They probably want me to kill someone."

"How would you feel about that very thing?" he asked.

My reaction was matter of fact. "When I was in the marines 'busting my cherry' was all I lived for. I was treated like an outcast until I proved I could do it. Now it don't mean nothin'. I've done my share of killing already, but if more has to be done, well, that's showbiz," I said.

He looked at me and repeated my comment, "That's showbiz," and snickered. We understood each other from that moment on.

He then explained to me that hiring killers was easy but that I had one extra qualification for the job—I was a young Canadian citizen who had the look of Teutonic breeding that was required for one specific job. He didn't elaborate on the mission but he did say that there would be a very generous financial package at its successful completion.

He went on to say that first I would need to undergo months of multi-disciplinary development before I was ready, and the training had already begun. I was dismissed in the same manner as the previous day and the door opened and in walked the guard. He motioned for me to follow and I stood up and waited until I received the officer's attention and I snapped him a salute. He returned it and I did an about face and marched out the door.

The routine was the same as the day before. After my shower I was back in my cell. I attended to my push-ups and sit-ups and then, lying on my back, I began to construct my chessboard. The files, the ranks, and then the diagonals. Now I started to place the chessmen on the board. First I tried to place the white queen rook on the board and work my way across the file to the other white king rook but became confused. I worked at this until I fell asleep.

I was awakened for lunch. By now I could tell when there was movement outside my cell door; the slightest shuffling of the guard's feet was a signal that someone was out there. I could time it when the first sound of the keys would jingle and then when they were placed into the lock. The sound was always the same. Then the door would open and standing there were the two guards.

"Have you guys got names?" I asked. All I got was the signal to hand over my empty tray and accept the full one. The guard would always back out of the cell like I was some kind of a wild animal and close the door behind him, turn the tumblers in the lock, and then silence.

I ate my meal and then went back to my push-up, sit-up routine. I was still very sore but I noticed that after the first ten or so push-ups the pain would go away and free me up to add more to my total. After that I began to pace back and forth. I continued the pacing for about an hour and then flopped on the cot and began again to construct my chessboard.

This was only the third day but I could see that by being confined I was able to draw on an ability to concentrate that I didn't know I possessed. Again I had to start from the beginning and work myself to where I had left off a few hours before. This time I tried a different approach. I place the rooks at the four corners of the board. This way I could establish the rook files in my mind, from one end of the board to the other. The hardest part was coloring them. I worked at this until I fell asleep.

The next morning I was awake when I first heard the scuffling outside the floor, the key in the lock, the tumblers turning, and the door opening. I was ready at the door this morning with my tray in hand. We exchanged trays in silence and I started my day's routine. At around 0:800 the door opened and I was signaled to follow the guards again. The routine was the same—one in front, one behind, down the corridor, up the steps, and out of the building. Mentally I counted the number of steps and the number of stairs.

We headed in a different direction than we had the previous days and entered a different building. I was ushered into a classroom and instructed to sit at a desk. It was like any other classroom I had been in, with about twenty desks and a blackboard. After a few minutes a female in uniform entered through the same door that I had entered. As with the officer who had been interviewing me the previous two days, there was no indication of rank or unit on her uniform. She introduced herself in a heavy Sabra accent and sat down at what reminded me of the teacher's desk of any school I had ever attended.

She began to question me about explosives and wanted to know everything I knew about them and wrote down everything I said. I told her my training was limited to Claymores, which were standard in the U.S. military, and hand grenades. She asked me what I knew about plastic explosives and detonators. I explained that I had never been trained in that kind of explosives and I believed that training was limited to Special Forces. My training was pretty much actual combat.

She then stood in front of the blackboard and began to draw some diagrams of what she was going to teach me over the next few weeks. She said that it would all seem very sophisticated at first but I would get it after a while. She wrote down the names of several explosives, some which resemble the American standard C-4, but the list went on. The first lesson lasted most of the morning. She went over and over certain things and then after looking at her watch she stopped and left the room. The back door opened, the guard called me out, and we returned to the building I was calling home.

We continued the same routine, down the corridor to the shower room, having my shower in full view of my guards, and then picking up my lunch tray off the food cart and back into my cell.

I ate my meal, did my push-ups and sit-ups, and paced the room. I then lay on my back and began to construct my chessboard.

It was a little easier this time. My eyes went straight up to the spot I had picked out. I was now getting a routine: first the files, then the ranks, and then the diagonals. When I had completed that I started with my four rooks around the board and then I colored them. I went over and over them before I introduced the knights. It wasn't any easier but I just kept at it. I would look with my eyes open and then shut, painting the picture in my mind, over and over, until I fell asleep.

The shuffling of the boots outside my door woke me up again. The familiarity was almost welcome. We marched back across the compound into the classroom and again waiting for me was my instructor with more lessons on explosives. This particular routine carried on for a couple of weeks and I felt myself becoming like a robot. I had the chessboard complete in my mind and had managed to developed the knight-before-bishop opening that I had learned back at the kibbutz. I was also becoming very proficient at the fundamentals of making bombs of every kind and how to detonate them in very sophisticated ways.

One morning before exiting the building I was handed a uniform to put on along with regulation boots. When we walked out of the door to make our way across the compound, a van was parked in front of the building and I was ordered to climb in. First the guard, then me in the middle, and the other guard next to the door. My instructor was sitting in the passenger seat and another man in uniform was behind the wheel. We drove out of the compound and into the city traffic.

I felt like a bear emerging from hibernation. We drove past apartments and shops with people attending to the normal duties of life. After we had only driven a short way I was feeling like there was nothing normal about my life. We then made our way out of the city.

I couldn't tell where we were when, after a couple of hours of driving, we arrived at a military base of some kind. After a thorough inspection by the guards at the gate we drove past them and onto the base. It reminded me of an American army base but without a name. Every one of the American military bases I had been on had a big sign indicating where you were and which outfit occupied the ground you were standing on.

We passed several military looking buildings and kept on driving for several miles until we stopped at what turned out to be an explosives range. We proceeded to make bombs and detonate them. We only stopped for lunch, when we all piled into the van and drove back across the base to one of the buildings that turned out to be a mess hall. I filed in with the rest of the soldiers and no one inside took any notice of me. The place was full of military personnel speaking Hebrew and I kept my mouth shut and observed. I stood in line with the rest and when my tray was full I sat and ate with my instructor. How something as common as sitting and eating lunch could feel so good amazed me.

When we finished eating we filed back to the van and drove back across the base and began blowing up more bombs. They must have raided the local dump because we blew up about twenty old refrigerators that day. This was the most fun I had had in months and I was really sad when we all climbed back into the van and headed back into the city. Before getting into the vehicle I ripped a small leafy weed up by the roots and jammed it into my pocket. I wanted so badly to feel something alive and green. I took it back to my cell and placed it in some water in my sink and enjoyed its presence.

We repeated the same procedure for the next week. I was always up and ready to go when my door was opened in the morning. I couldn't have been happier, building bombs and blowing things up. This was every kid's dream, it was like Hallowe'en every day and we kept it up until I was an explosives expert.

When it was decided I was proficient in the art of making bombs, they changed my routine. In the morning instead of climbing into the van I was marched across the parade square into another building which housed a small gymnasium. My guards, who would change from week to week and were never friendly to me, now had a chance to show what their specialties were. I was given a karate uniform and told to change into it while one of my guards did the same. I was really glad I had taken the time to stay in shape doing my push-ups and sit-ups but soon realized my cardio was going to let me down. I happily accepted the head gear that was offered to me, having visions of Staff Sergeant Mejia kicking the shit out of me at boot camp.

The guard motioned me to the center of a mat that was on the floor and basically challenged me to show him what I had. He was better than good; he did not, however, have a seventeen-year-old recruit like Staff Sergeant Mejia had to kick around. We sparred for about an hour until I could hardly stand up and the guard looked almost as fresh as when we had started. He had a good sweat built up but nothing like mine.

After our workout I was allowed to shower and get back into my jumpsuit before being marched back across the compound, through the door, and down the corridor and into my cell. I lay down on my bed and tried to picture my chessboard but was much too tired and fell asleep until I heard the familiar shuffling at the door. When it opened and my meal tray was pushed in on the floor it sat undisturbed until it was cold. When I finally got up to eat I could feel a stiffness setting in and I ate the cold meal and went right back to sleep.

When I woke up the next morning I had never been so stiff or in so much pain in my life. It was an effort just to get up out of bed. Usually I was happy to hear the keys jingle and the door open. It was usually a real highlight, but on this morning I could have done without it. Nevertheless, the door opened at 0:800 and I was marched across the compound and into the gym. This time it was the other guard who changed his clothes and motioned me onto the mat. I was much slower this day and I hesitated. I began to stall and for a few minutes did some stretching before I slowly walked onto the mat. After I warmed up and got my heartbeat up I was OK and started to enjoy myself. I even got a couple good licks in before we ended our session.

As on the previous day, I showered in the gym, marched back across the compound, through the doors, down the corridor, picked up my food tray, and was locked in. I can't explain why I put up with this treatment but I did. On this, my second day of hand-to-hand training, I wasn't as stiff and I continued my chess game. I was getting so I could arrange the board and the players in a very short time but was still stuck on my opening.

We continued this routine always in silence and it was driving me crazy, so I began to taunt my opponents when we were sparring. I would talk to them knowing their English was perfect but there was never a response.

After a few days of hand-to-hand training one of the guards produced a rubber knife. I was startled when he said to me in English, "Ever use one of these?" and gave me a wink.

"Who's doing the taunting now?" I said and tried unsuccessfully to disarm him.

I was beginning to grow in confidence, just as I had back in boot camp. And now I knew I had an advantage over these two, who for the past two months had treated me like an animal. The guards were technically perfect but they didn't have the "look" in their eyes. "I'll bet you've never even used one of these," I said. "Do you want to know what it sounds like when it goes in?" I asked. "Better yet, do you know what it smells like? You're probably nothing but a fuckin' cherry boy." I was really feeling my oats this morning but soon realized I didn't know much about knife fighting.

The guard really knew his stuff but he couldn't instruct me in silence so he took me through my paces with expertise. It made me feel foolish for my insensitive remark, but this was knife fighting, I reminded myself, and he was teaching me how to kill. I spent a good part of that morning on my back on the mat with the rubber knife across my throat.

Back in my cell my routine was the same: push-ups, sit-ups, pacing back and forth, and then my chessboard on the ceiling. I was still stuck on my opening. I couldn't just jump in. I had to go through the process one step at a time until I had the chessmen all on the board and was ready for my first transfer. Every time I got to this point I would hear in the back of my mind the kibbutznick who had first introduced me to the game. "Making a move is a duty and a privilege." Then I would make my first move. The same thing then happened every day. I would hear his voice again. "Each chessman is moved and captured according to the powers laid down for it." As though he was reading it out of a book. I now began to believe that all the memorizing I had done as a child must have trained my brain to remember his voice. It was weird, but I was living inside my head, and being confined in this cell was encouraging that ability.

My knife fighting instruction along with the rigorous hand-to-hand training was making me sharp. This went on for nearly a month until I could hold my own with my instructors. If and when I ever needed these skills, my victims wouldn't stand a chance. The addition of the element of surprise would make it all be over in a matter of seconds.

Again one morning one of the guards stopped me before I could exit my cell and told me to put on the uniform and boots. When we emerged from my dungeon there was the van parked in front of the door. I was motioned in and again we went through the same routine, one guard on each side, and away we drove out of the gates and into the city traffic. The only difference from my last trip outside the gates was my explosives teacher wasn't on board.

What a feeling! I took everything in, the people on the streets, the cars, the trees along the boulevards, everything. I was on a high.

I recognized the route we were on and I was not surprised when we pulled up to the gate at the explosives range. In we went, but instead of driving to the place where we set off all the bombs we drove to another part of the base, which turned out to be the rifle range.

We got out and walked over to the firing line. On a table were several types of rifles I had never seen before along with a couple I recognized. The rifles were all in cases and were broken down. I first had to learn how to assemble the rifles one by one before I was given a chance to fire them. The first rifle I was given to fire was a .308 with a 9x scope. I had never had much training with a scope but I was such a good marksman that it didn't matter. I could tell my guards were impressed. This is where I shone.

Off in the background was the guard with the Uzi and he seemed to be on high alert. After trying to kick the shit out of me for the past couple of months I think his trust of me was very limited or nonexistent, but he was impressed. We all took turns firing the .308, exchanging ideas on wind and light, trajectory of the bullet, the grain of the ammunition. We only stopped for lunch when we went back to the mess hall and again ate with all the soldiers. After our meal we headed back out to the firing range.

It was a really good outing and it ended too soon. When it was time to get back in the van and head back to my cell one of the guards could see I didn't want to go and for the first time in months he showed a tiny bit of compassion. "Don't worry, we are coming back tomorrow," he said and my face must have lit up. I knew I had a grin from ear to ear.

The next day was much of the same, assembling the .308, firing a number of rounds at still and moving targets, and disassembling the weapon. This went on all day with only a break for lunch, which was the same as the day before. The afternoon of the second day I didn't fire the weapon at all. A company of soldiers were marched over to our position and began there own target practice. My earplugs were taken away from me and I was blindfolded and made to assemble and disassemble the weapons. The noise was meant to disrupt my concentration and it worked. My ears were ringing and I was in a bad mood all the way back to my cell.

We were back on the range the next day but along with the rifles there were a number of handguns. There were revolvers, automatics, and sub-machine guns. There were dozens of different types: 9mm, 22mm, there was even an old U.S. Colt .45. We started at one end of the table. I was handed a revolver, told to empty it at a target, and then place it back on the table. I fired every pistol on the table and soon learned I was really a lousy shot with a handgun. I had never had any extensive training with handguns and only carried one once on mission in Vietnam. Side arms were reserved for officers in the U.S. Marines except recon marines and I wasn't with them long enough to get proficient.

They called in a special instructor for me that day and we went over the weapons. I was fitted with holsters and made to do fast draws like in the old Wild West. The holsters, however, were not the cowboy type. One was fitted on my leg and I practiced pulling out the weapon and firing it as fast as I could. Then I was trained how to pull and fire from out of my belt. I was then taught the proper way to brandish a weapon from behind my back and come out firing. My hand and wrist was sore by the time we called it a day.

When I became competent in all aspects of firing handguns, my training took on another phase. One day we didn't take the usual turn and drive across the base to the firing range. Instead, we took another route and drove to a huge parking lot that looked like a giant obstacle course. There was a car waiting with its engine running and I was loaded into it and given a tour through the obstacle course as fast as the car would go. It was a very powerful European sedan. This will be the ride of a lifetime, I thought. When we finally came to a stop the instructor told me I would have to be able to complete the course in the same amount of time he just did. I had never even had a ride in a car like that sedan, let alone been allowed to drive.

We exchanged seats and my driver training began. I had a driver's license from back in Canada but never really drove anything but my father's old pickup truck. I had a lot to learn. The first time around the track I was constantly corrected by the instructor. This was not the usual silent treatment I had received up until now. He spoke constantly and it was unnerving. At one point I stopped the car and got out and made him get in the driver's seat and do the driving. I told him he was going to have to take it easy on me, that this was really pissing me off, this was new to me, and he was going to have to be patient. "We are not children here," he told me and sped off around the track.

That was the first time I had stood up to anyone at all up to this point. In my hand-to-hand combat training I got to get a few licks in but it was in the heat of battle. This guy really got on my nerves and I felt like just grabbing one of the handguns and shooting him. I didn't realize it then but all the training I was going through was leading me up to a point where I would be able to assassinate someone and not even think twice. For whatever reason their political masters deemed necessary I was being trained to act without thinking.

After he drove around the course one more time he ordered me behind the wheel. I climbed back in the driver's seat and began to drive the course again. I drove the car at my own pace for the rest of the day, putting up with the instructor's nonstop abuse. At one point I looked over and saw a 9mm automatic in his belt and knew I better cool it. I could tell this guy didn't like me and the feeling was mutual. I also noticed he was unlike the other instructors—he had the look in his eyes and I knew he wouldn't hesitate to pull out his gun and shoot me if he had the slightest reason. When the time came to climb back in the van and drive back to the city, I could hear him talking to my guards and from the little bit of Hebrew I could understand, I knew he was telling them that I would never be able to complete the course. I looked over at him and couldn't hold back. "Fuck you," I said and he just looked back with an icy stare.

On the way back into the city I asked my guards what his name was. They had a real chuckle but refused to answer me. "That guy's a real prick, isn't he?" I said. I couldn't hold it back. He had really gotten under my skin. "Can't you guys get me another instructor?" I asked. They chuckled again and we continued our drive back into Tel Aviv.

The next day we pulled up in the van and there was the same instructor leaning on the car. I got out of the van and walked over to the car and he gave me a smile. In his hand he had a set of earplugs, which he offered to me and I gladly accepted. "I hear you don't like to listen to me so you can have these," he said and gave me a friendly wink. Before we climbed into the car he instructed me to open all the windows and then to drive to a certain spot as fast as I could, come to a screeching stop, and reverse my direction and come back here.

With that, we climbed into the car and proceeded down the course. When I hit the brakes and came to a rolling stop he pulled out his automatic and began firing out the window at a target that was set up. I could feel the bullets as they passed by my nose and the sound was deafening. With one last bullet in the chamber he grabbed me by my collar and stuck the gun under my chin. The barrel was still smoking and burned my flesh. He then screamed into my ear, "You are nothing but a fucking mercenary, you know nothing about our struggle! I should kill you right here and now!"

I proceeded to piss my pants.

He told me to get out of the car and walk back to the starting point. I got out of the car with my wet clothes and while I tried to soothe the burn under my chin I walked back to where the van was parked. He followed behind. My guards loaded me up and took me back to a building beside the dining hall where I was allowed to take a shower and change my clothes. His words were burning in my mind. After the shower the guards produced some cleaning products, a bucket, and some rags, then drove me back to the car. I was instructed to clean up the mess and then drive the car back to the starting point. I was humiliated and my neck was stinging where he had placed the hot barrel of his gun. I was ready to have it out with this guy. I was starting to feel too good about myself to allow this to happen. It was all part of the training but I was so caught up in it that I didn't realize what was going on. I filed this moment away for a later date.

They didn't allow me any time to feel sorry for myself. We both climbed back into the car and continued the day's training. We drove around the course the rest of the morning and he never let up for a moment. I had to hold myself back from reaching into his belt and grabbing his gun and blowing a hole in his head when we broke for lunch. I stopped the car where the van was parked and we all climbed in and drove to the mess hall. "I think you are going to get the hang of this," he said as we drove across the base.

Back in my cell that night I began to wonder what this was all leading up to. The training was intense with absolutely no indication of a mission, only that I was being trained to be some kind of automatic assassin.

We continued the high-speed driver training for several weeks. I was eventually supplied with a handgun and trained to fire from the speeding car. This was a juvenile delinquent's dream, driving down the road shooting out of the window of the car. It was not as simple as it would seem; racing a car down a course and judging the trajectory of a bullet is extremely difficult. It took me forever to pass the test but I eventually did.

All the time this was going on and all the time I had spent on the kibbutz I had never had the occasion to read a newspaper or listen to a radio. Not that it would have made any difference. I couldn't understand the radio and couldn't read the newspaper. During my short stay in West Virginia I had never picked up a paper or watched a news report either. I was in fact totally ignorant of world affairs. I had heard about the massacre at the Olympic village in Munich a couple of years before and how a number of Israeli athletes were killed in a botched rescue attempt but never gave it much thought. It had left the entire world in a state of shock and brought the Israeli—Arab conflict to the forefront of the world scene. When I was swept up by Golda Meir's speech on that October morning in 1973 I never thought for a moment that these events were all interconnected. I was still totally caught up in my own world trying to come to terms with my own war experience. I could never have dreamed that these events would ever have any affect on my life.

It was after about five months of training that I was marched into the building where I had had my first interview. Sitting at the same desk as if he had never moved was the same officer, chain smoking the same kind of cigarette and looking down at what I presumed was the same file. Today the file was much larger; in fact, the stack of papers was quite high. I assumed that my guards and instructors must have had to file daily reports on my progress. I was feeling a lot more confident than that day when I had first entered this room. I was in good physical condition and I had become quite skilled in the art of killing. I had even learned to live inside of my head with my chess exercises.

The officer was a lot friendlier on this occasion; he asked me lots of questions, looking up periodically from his desk. He asked me what I thought all this training was intended for and my reply was succinct. "You want me to kill someone," I answered without any hesitation.

"And do you have a problem with that?" was his reply.

My answer to that question was easy. "Nope," I said.

Then the conversation took on a different tone. We understood each other perfectly. I was no longer a recruit, I was his assassin. I had chosen to stay when I could have quit at any time. I had been treated like an animal at times and never once shown any kindness. For over five months I had been subjected to almost total silence. I had taken everything they could throw at me and passed the test. I was ready to do my master's bidding. I could kill quickly and efficiently with everything from a sniper's rifle to a letter bomb. I could kill from a speeding vehicle or with an injection of poison. I could kill in close with a knife or use only bare hands. I had become a very dangerous man.

The officer began to talk about the Munich Olympics and how the men that had committed these horrendous acts had to be brought to justice. I immediately thought of Golda's speech, "An eye for an eye and a tooth for a tooth." My mind raced back to my exacting revenge on the Protestant boys for disparaging the priests and the nuns when I was a child and how I still felt betrayed by my religion. I listened intently as he began to unravel a story. He asked, "Have you ever heard of Lillehammer?"

I said that the word meant nothing to me.

He went on to explain that it was a city in Norway and intelligence had tracked a leader of the Munich massacre to this city. He went on to say that some months ago he had personally sent a team there to take this man out. The team members had used Canadian passports and were rather sloppy in their intelligence gathering and preparation and the entire mission was compromised when they took out the wrong target. Subsequently the entire recovery team was arrested and they were still sitting in a prison in Norway. "This has become somewhat of a diplomatic embarrassment between my government and the Canadian government," he said.

I was wondering what this could possibly have to do with me when he asked just that question and answered it himself. "Now we have received intelligence that two more of the people involved have made their way to Canada and are in hiding within the Lebanese community in Montreal. These targets must be dealt with, but this time we must have better logistics, preparation, and a successful conclusion with no mistakes." He said that because of my appearance, language skills, and citizenship I could be a valuable asset to the team that he was preparing for this mission.

While he was telling me this story it struck me that if I didn't accept his conditions I would probably never leave that room alive. He told me that because I was only going to be used for this one mission and I would be paid a large sum of money at its conclusion, I would be required to keep my mouth shut. If I ever opened my mouth I would probably spend the rest of my life in prison for murder or worse. When he said the words "or worse" I got the message loud and clear. This was not the first time I had my life threatened by someone who had the means to carry it out.

"Now before we go any further," he said, "do you foresee any problems with your participation in this mission?"

"Not from me," I said.

"Good," was his reply.

Things changed that day. I wasn't escorted to my cell like a criminal. I was taken to another part of the compound and shown into an apartment. It had a real bed, not just a cot and a desk, and there was an attached bathroom. There was even a television set which I immediately turned on and stared at from the edge of the bed. It was all in Hebrew but I didn't care. I was mesmerized. There was no shuffle of feet in the corridor, no jingle of keys, and no tumblers turning in a lock. I got up off the bed and opened the door and looked up and down the hall just to be sure I wasn't dreaming. I was giddy. There was also a change of clothes, a uniform laid out on the bed. I immediately got out of the jumpsuit. I had been wearing jumpsuits for months and couldn't get out of this one fast enough. I then went into the bathroom and had a shower in private. After toweling off I put on the uniform and again sat on the edge of the bed and looked at the television.

After a couple of hours there was a knock at the door. This was the strangest part of the whole day. I sheepishly got up off the bed and answered the door. At first I opened it just a crack and peeked out. Standing in the doorway was one of my guards. He looked me in the eyes and in perfect English told me that I was required to attend a meeting in one hour. I was a little stunned and replied, "Ya, OK, I'll be ready," and closed the door. I walked over to the bed and lay down on my back. My first reaction was to start in with my chessboard but instead I closed my eyes and went to sleep.

There was another knock on the door that woke me up. I jumped up and assumed a defensive posture. I had been dreaming and it took a few seconds to get my bearings. I looked around the room and it all came back to me. A little embarrassed I opened the door and there was my guard. He politely asked me to follow him.

We walked over to the building that housed the classroom I had attended for my explosives training. I was escorted as far as the door. The guard knocked on the door and motioned me to enter. I walked through the door not knowing what to expect next but it didn't matter. I was in the best mood I had been in since I entered into this program. I walked in through that back door as always and sitting in the room with their backs to me were seven people, five men and two women. They were all in uniform and no one bothered to turn around and look. I found an empty desk and sat down. After several minutes of silence the officer who had initially interviewed me entered the room and walked to the front of the class. He had a file folder in his hand and he placed it on the desk and began speaking in Hebrew. He pointed his finger at me while he was speaking and everyone in the class turned and looked at me. I couldn't understand much of what he was saying but I got the message loud and clear.

The thing I noticed first was that every one of the men looked like they came out of the same mold. They looked Middle Eastern and I recognized one of them. It was my driving instructor. He winked at me and said, "Shalom."

I looked away and said, "Oh shit." I still had a welt under my chin where he had burned me with his handgun and I was still pissed at him over it.

All the faces were given names but I instantly forgot them. The only one I remembered was my driving instructor, who was introduced as Ben. I also noticed that the two female officers were extremely attractive. After the introductions everyone turned back toward the front of the class. The only other thing that struck my attention was that I was by far the youngest person in the room. I had been in Israel long enough to tell the difference between veterans of the Yom Kippur War and veterans of the Six Day War. They were totally different generations. I likened it to the difference between the Beatles generation and the Elvis generation back home in Canada.

The instructor then opened the file folder and passed around some photographs. Everyone studied them carefully and passed them on. I was handed the pictures last. They were surveillance photos of a man and a woman in what looked like a Middle Eastern city. None of the pictures were very clear, some were with the two people together and some were in crowds of people with the two highlighted. We were told that these were our targets.

The instructor went on to explain why it was believed that after Munich they had made their way to Canada, Montreal in particular, and were in hiding there. He said they had not been located yet and that would be our task. We were to travel to Montreal, set up in several apartments, acquire the targets, and take them out. There was to be no trace of our team ever being there. All our assignments would be carefully laid out but we would be expected to use any and all means available to us. My job in particular would be to furnish vehicles, rent apartments, and provide any support necessary. My first assignment was to fly back to New York and then attend gun shows and purchase a number of weapons that were readily available in the United States but almost impossible to find in Canada. He stressed that any and all equipment had to be either purchased or made in North America. We would only use explosives as a last resort. It would be my job to smuggle the guns into Canada and supply them to members of the team.

He then went on to say "This mission is not going to be a repeat of Lillehammer." You could feel the tension in the room when he mentioned that name. I didn't know it but that situation was far from settled and I was to learn later that the agents who were captured on that mission were familiar to this group.

We went over detail after detail before breaking for lunch. We filed out of the room as a team. For the others it might have been like another day at the office but for me it was like the first day of my new life. Even though our mission was ghastly I was walking on a cloud.

I was used to eating alone except when we were at the firing range. Today was different. I lined up with all the rest in a large dining room and subsequently sat with the team at a table. The room was full of men and women, some in uniform, some in civvies. The chatter reminded me of the kibbutz. I could pick out words referring to what I thought must have been basketball teams but it was fuzzy. I had been locked away for so long I didn't know if it was basketball season or soccer season. My team was not saying a word; they were polite but I could sense that they didn't trust me a bit. Ben was the only one who spoke to me and he just mocked me about the welt under my chin. I took it all in a humorous spirit and bantered back and forth with him as though we were talking about something that might have happened in a locker room at the end of a game. The other agents looked and listened and I even got a few glances from the females. I thought to myself that they must have been picked for their beauty because they couldn't be competent at the mission at hand. I would learn later that their good looks had nothing to do with the way they handled their duties.

After our meal we met in the classroom for the rest of that day and when we ended our meeting my guard appeared at the door and, as always, I was escorted out of the room but now it was to my new lodgings. Once back in my room I turned on the television and stared into the screen. In a couple of hours there was a knock on the door and my guard, who I guessed by now wasn't going to ever be far away, said it was dinnertime. We walked together over to the dining hall and it was not as busy as lunchtime. He sat with me and we ate together. Even this was a shock to my system. I was obviously still in his care but everything was eased off just a bit.

After dinner we walked back to my apartment and he informed me that I was to remain in my room until he retrieved me in the morning. He said there would be a guard in front of the building and I would likely be shot if I wandered out without permission.

The team met again the next day. We went over and over every scenario we could think of. Ben was always on my case. One time he spoke up and said, "This guy doesn't even speak French, what help can he be?" It was obvious that there was going to be tension between us until this was over and in the end I wasn't sure how we would settle our differences. If it was up to me I would have really enjoyed just shooting him on the spot and I wondered if it would come to that. After about a week I started to get to know the rest of the team and I especially liked it when the females showed me a little attention

This routine carried on for two more weeks when it was decided we were as ready as we were going to be. I would be the first one to go to North America and begin to put things in place. I was told I was to be accompanied by another member of the team but just who this would be wasn't made clear.

I sure hope it isn't Ben, I thought to myself.

I was told I still had time left on my return ticket to New York and would be required to travel there alone. I was asked to pick a location where I could meet up with my other team members. New York, I said to myself. I didn't have a clue about New York. I had driven in on a bus and climbed aboard the airport shuttle, drove through the city to the airport, and flew out. I didn't know what to say when all of a sudden it came to me. On the kibbutz my chess mate used to talk about a park in Greenwich Village where New Yorkers played outdoor chess matches. It was probably the most famous place in the world for chess, he told me. He said some of the best chess hustlers in the world hung out there and it was his dream to be able to go there.

"Washington Park Square," I said without reservation, "at the chess circle," and the first decision of my new life was made.

Before leaving for New York there was the matter of my compensation, and I mentioned it out loud in the meeting that day. It was met with silence by the other members of the team. This showed what I really was and how I would be treated. I was nothing more than a hired killer and I could see it in their eyes, the way they looked at me. They had begun to be friendlier with me after the past week but that ended when I spoke out that morning. These people were here for one reason, and it was now obvious I was here for another.

I met with the officer in charge that same afternoon. He was sitting at his desk and I was invited to sit in the same chair I had sat in some six months before. He was chain smoking cigarettes as before and going over my file. He told me that no one thought I would be able to finish the six-month program, not being Jewish, and obviously having a personality disorder.

"What's with this personality disorder?" I asked angrily.

He said my behavior showed I was too easily influenced, and it could have got me killed back on the kibbutz. He did go on to say that I had performed very well since I had been there and he felt I would be able to accomplish the mission.

"You will be paid $20,000 up front and another $20,000 when the mission is completed," he said. "You will be given some traveling money and when you reach New York you are to go to the Chase Manhattan Bank in the Chase Plaza and open an account." The money would be transferred to that account. He said that my other team member would provide the funds for all the logistical support that would be required to accomplish the mission.

He stood up and offered me his hand and wished me God's speed and good luck. I stood up, walked up to his desk, reached over and shook his hand and told him I wouldn't disappoint him. I turned and walked to the door and opened it. Before I walked out of his office I turned and asked him a question.

"What is the name of this organization?"

He replied, "We are Mossad."

CHAPTER EIGHT

The next day my clothes were returned to me and I was driven into Tel Aviv to a barber shop and given a haircut. For some reason that was the one thing that was absent in all my training. After cleaning up I was then driven to the airport and handed my passport, my return ticket to New York, and an envelope with one thousand American dollars. I was instructed to get a room in a certain hotel in Greenwich Village and go to the park every day until I was contacted.

I felt like a secret agent. I had seen a few movies about this kind of thing but never imagined I would ever be involved in something top secret. While I was waiting for my flight I found a spy novel in the airport bookstore and began reading it. My mind started to race. I had never been much of a reader but my mind had been trained by my chess exercises. I began to devour the book. I had to wait in the airport for all of that day and part of the next before I was able to get a seat on a flight. I sat and read most of that time.

Once in the air I began to realize the enormity of what was going on in my life and wondered if it was all real. I lost myself in the book and started to take on the personality of the hero until in the end of the book where the hero was betrayed and killed and it struck me: was that what was in store for me? It had been made very clear to me that I was only going to be needed for this one operation and then retired. I gave that scenario a lot of thought and knew it would be a pleasure for Ben to kill me. I made up my mind right then that I would have to really watch myself.

The flight landed in New York late in the evening and after passing through customs I gathered up my backpack and walked out of the terminal looking for a taxi. It was June in New York City and even though it was a lot cooler than Tel Aviv the temperature was nice and fresh. Even late at night the place was buzzing. I hopped into a taxi and gave the driver the name of the hotel in Greenwich Village and struck up a conversation with him. "It's not too far from Washington Square Park," he told me. Most of the hotels around there were pretty expensive, he said, but the one I was going to on Seventeenth Street was reasonable and about a mile from Union Square.

I was exhausted after the flight, all the reading, and everything that had happened in the past year. I was a different person from the young man who had been swept up in delusional patriotism and jetted off to an unknown fate. I had been involved in a situation that in any other circumstances might have landed me in prison for the rest of my life. It did, however, provide the criteria for the next phase of my life that couldn't be scripted by a Hollywood writer. The eight months I had spent in Vietnam, however traumatic, were in no way comparable to the influence of the last eight months. I came back from Vietnam with a scar on my neck and a medal and no prospects at all. This time I was returning with a purpose, an assassin on a deadly mission.

The taxi dropped me off at the hotel and there was a room available. I paid for a week in advance, caught the elevator, found my room, and climbed into bed. It was a great sleep and when I awoke I looked out at New York City. I stood at the window and just stared out. I was in a kind of shock. Only a week before I was living like a caged animal, everything taken care of for me. Now I had to plan breakfast. I never knew how such a trivial matter could confuse me so. I climbed back into bed but it was no use. I couldn't sleep. I had to get up and face the day. I had my shower, and then noticed I had no toiletries in my pack, so along with breakfast, a trip to a drugstore was my next priority. When I stepped onto the sidewalk in front of the hotel I was struck by the movement and the action. Everything appeared to be moving at mach one. People were everywhere and all on the move. I became a face in the crowd and began to walk. Along with breakfast and a trip to the drugstore I also had to find out which way to Washington Square Park and the bank. I turned around and walked back to my hotel and asked the person at the desk which way to the park and was pointed in the right direction.

On my first walk on the streets of Manhattan I must have looked like the typical tourist in New York for the first time. I was in awe of the atmosphere, and the closer I got to the park the more I became excited to see one of the most famous chess venues in the world. When I arrived at the chess circle lots of games were already going on. Crowds were gathered around some of the tables and everywhere there were people coming and going. I mingled with the crowd and watched a game in progress. It was the first time I had laid my eyes on a chessboard in months.

At first glance my mind shot back to all the hours I had spent on my back looking up into the blank ceiling, creating my own imaginary chessboard. I thought to myself that I would never miss that place.

I tried to follow the game but it was impossible. I couldn't believe how fast they were playing. They would move and punch the clock, move and punch the clock. It made me dizzy and I had to look away. I had to walk over to a bench and sit down to collect myself. I was still feeling the effects of my incarceration.

I wasn't seated for long before I was invited to play a game for a couple of dollars. I politely declined; one part of me wanted to play a game but another part of me told me I wasn't ready. I did, however, ask how to get to Chase Plaza and was pointed in the right direction. When my dizziness left me I began the long walk from Greenwich Village to Chase Plaza. It was quite an experience—I could never have dreamed that this kind of place existed. It took me hours to finally come to my destination, only stopping along the way to buy a hotdog from a street vendor. I was exhausted. My cardio was just not up to any acceptable standard. I had gone through months of sparring in the gym but my legs were weak. I was just in no shape to even go into the bank when I finally found the entrance; instead I hailed a taxi and asked to be taken back to my hotel. Once back in my room I fell asleep on my bed and didn't wake up until late in the evening.

So this is what jet lag is, I thought when I woke up. I tried to get back to sleep but it was no use. I got up, left my room, and walked down the stairs to the lobby feeling hungry again. I went outside and found another street vendor and bought another hotdog and began to walk down the street. It wasn't as busy as during the day but this truly was "the city that never sleeps." I walked until I was getting sleepy and then returned to my hotel and went back to bed. I was determined to get to sleep but I tossed and turned until the daylight started to appear in the window.

When I awakened it was almost noon. I couldn't ever remember sleeping in this late. I got up, had a long shower, and without brushing my teeth I left the hotel with the intention of finding a drugstore and then to walk to Chase Plaza again. Out on the street I fell into the ranks of the crowd. Everyone was moving at a pace I had trouble keeping up with. I began to feel paranoid, all these people and where could they all be going? This time I made it to the bank and waited in line for over an hour. When it was my turn I opened an account as I had been instructed to do and then walked back to Washington Square Park and to the chess circle. I joined the crowd watching a game, staying for several hours before walking back to my hotel and falling asleep again.

My jet lag lasted about a week until I could sleep at night and get up in the morning. My routine was one of walking from the hotel to the bank and back to the park. My diet consisted of street vendor food. Every day I would walk to the bank and stand in line only to be told there was no money in my account. I would then walk back to the park and watch some chess matches, not having the confidence yet to try to take on any of the hustlers who invited me to play. I was on a constant watch for anyone I could recognize but no one appeared. I finally found a bookstore and bought another spy thriller and began to read about secret agents. If I was going to be a secret agent I thought I should read about how to go about it.

As the days dragged on and there was no contact I began to feel that I might have been forgotten about or just written off as a bad experiment. After a couple of weeks of this routine and still no money in my bank account I began to get concerned about my situation. I hadn't spent any money on anything but living expenses, but this city wasn't cheap and I was running out of money. I then did something I wished I hadn't. I found a movie theatre that was playing the movie "Midnight Cowboy" and bought a ticket and went in. This movie had won some academy awards a couple years earlier and I had heard somewhere that it was a movie about New York City. When the movie was over and I walked back out on the street I felt so depressed that I started to make plans to leave the city. My spy novels had no provisions for what I was going through. There was always nonstop action and support in the books. I, on the other hand, was feeling abandoned. I began to think that they must have received new intelligence. Perhaps the targets were not in North America after all and the mission had been cancelled. The contempt that the team felt for me made me think that I would be forgotten about so I decided to either make my way back to West Virginia or to Canada.

I didn't know what to do. I wondered if I could still take advantage of my veteran's benefits or if I had blown that opportunity. I was feeling really alone. When a month had gone by and still no contact and my money was almost gone I walked all the way to the bus depot and checked on the price of fare to West Virginia. I had come to believe my spy adventure was all behind me and I had to come back to the real world. I even began to think about getting a job.

And on top of it all, "Midnight Cowboy" had sent chills running down my spine. In the month I had been in the city I had run into the whole gamut of street hustlers but wasn't interested. I wasn't about to fall into the depth of depravity that the movie had shown could happen when you ran out of money in New York City. During the time I had been killing time in the park I was not only approached by the chess hustlers but had a number of fags come on to me, which was a new experience. I wasn't even polite to them, even threatening the life of one persistent queer. I was all but resigned to the realization that I was going to move out of the hotel and out of this city and forget about being a secret agent and write it all off as experience.

On my next visit to the park I finally got up the nerve to play one of the chess hustlers a match and was defeated in only a few moves. It didn't cost much and was a thrill. I wished I had played a match sooner because my time in New York was rapidly winding down. My daily walks had taken me all over the city and I had checked out much cheaper accommodations in different areas but decided I would give it a few more days before I made my move. I started to model my life after a chess game and was about to move my first pawn down the board.

When I had all but given up on my secret agent life I noticed a funny looking woman staring at me from one of the benches in the park. After she got my attention she walked over and sat down beside me. I thought she must be a cheap whore looking for a sucker. Her clothes were dirty, her blond hair a mess, she just looked like the junkie prostitutes who had propositioned me on a regular basis. I stood up to make my move when she said to me, *"Boker tov."* I stopped in my tracks and looked down at her. It took a few seconds to register. I hadn't heard a word of Hebrew in over a month and this tramp had just wished me a good morning.

Without thinking I answered her back, then sat down beside her and took a real good look at her. It was Ariela, one of the members of the team, and I didn't recognize her even up close. I had only been with her for a couple of weeks and had never talked directly to her. I had always been shy around women and in all of our meetings I never had any reason to speak to her and now here she was. Everything about her was different, her hair color, her clothes, and her demeanor; she just wasn't the same person. I told her that I had thought I had seen her before here in the park, and she said not only in the park. She produced a little booklet and began to read from it. She told me how many times I had attended the park. Then she went on to tell me how many times I had walked from my hotel to the bank. She told me on average how many minutes it took for my daily trip. She told me where I ate, and what I ate; the name of the books I had bought and was reading; the names of the movies I had attended. She indicated that she knew what kind of shaving cream and toothpaste I used and where I placed my toothbrush and razor after I used them. She then asked if I was planning on Canada or West Virginia for my trip.

I sat and listened until she had finished. I was speechless. "The rest of the team?" I asked, and she answered that some of the members had flown over a day before me to study my moves and the rest of the team followed a few days later. I told her I thought they had given up on me and I was almost broke.

"I want you to know that I can tell you right to the penny how much money you have." She added, "I know how many pages of your book you read in a day and the television programs you watch at night."

"You even bugged my room?" I said.

"Of course," was her reply.

"So what have you been doing, practicing on me or something?" I asked, and she just smiled.

She then handed me an envelope and said, "Here's some more money, you will be contacted," and she got up and walked away.

I couldn't watch any more chess that day. It struck me that these people were very good. I hadn't suspected a thing. They had been in my hotel room and watched every time I left the building. I supposed that they knew what time I went to sleep and got up in the morning. I sat on the bench going over my daily routine trying to picture anything odd. It was no use; they had undertaken a perfect surveillance and I had not been aware of anything. It was obvious that I was the amateur and they were the professionals. I got to thinking how easy it would be for them to terminate my participation in the mission and no one would ever know the difference. I then started to see how self-involved I had been in my little world of make-believe while they had been hard at work. What was the message that they were trying to get across to me? I wondered. One thing for sure I was glad of was the fact that I wasn't some kind of double agent. I would probably have already had a final run-in with my old friend Ben.

I decided the first thing I was going to do was find the bug in my hotel room. Walking back to the hotel I tried to see if I was being followed but it was impossible. If I gave up my concentration I would bump into some other pedestrian and get a New York welcome that was never pleasant. I decided it was impossible to try to pick up their surveillance so I continued on until I found a hardware store and stopped and bought a screwdriver that had all the different screw heads. I was determined to see if my room was bugged and if it was, I was going to dismantle the device.

I walked back to the hotel and up the stairs to my room. I always used the stairs. One reason was to keep in shape and the other was my phobia of elevators. In the first spy novel I read it seemed people were always getting bumped off in elevators and it put a real fear into me. When I got to my floor I waited at the top of the stairs and caught my breath before walking down the hallway. When I got to my door I opened it and entered as quietly as possible. Starting with the wall receptacles I began to unscrew the wall plates. One by one I took them off, not really knowing what I was looking for. I had not received any training in this field and thought I would just look for anything out of the ordinary. When I had all the top plates removed I could see that there was one with an extra part and more wires. I was convinced this was the bug and ripped it out of the wall. When I was in the process of removing the device it began to arc and sparks began to shoot out of the wall. I was startled and, not knowing anything about electricity, I stood back hoping I wasn't going to burn the hotel to the ground. As it turned out it only left a black mark on the wall that I wiped off. It probably tripped a breaker because none of the wall receptacles worked after that. I replaced all the receptacle covers and lay on the bed lost in my thoughts, staring at the little device that had been tracking my every move for over a month without my knowledge.

The next day after paying for my room for another week I didn't bother making my daily trek to the bank. I walked straight to the park and sat down at the chess circle looking around for someone to recognize. All the way to the park I would stop to see if I was being followed, looking for anything unusual. I saw nothing that would lead me to believe I was being followed or even watched. I sat for at least an hour before bothering to get into the mood of the place. I was invited to play a match and decided why not lose a couple of bucks. I was soundly beaten in the minimum number of moves and decided right there and then that I was being played just like the chess hustler was playing me. I was truly out of my league in both areas and if I was going to pull this thing off I was going to have to take on a new and professional attitude. I stayed at the park for several hours but was not contacted by anyone. I knew I must be under surveillance but couldn't pick anyone out in the crowd. I had the little listening device in my pocket and wanted to place it in Ariela's hand so badly but they were not about to give me the opportunity.

When I grew hungry and tired of waiting around the park I began my walk back to the hotel. I stopped by the bookstore and bought another spy novel with the intention that I was going to start thinking like a professional. Once back in my room I flopped on the bed and started reading. I read for the rest of the day and into the night, finally falling asleep. I woke up hungry late at night and decided to go down for a bite to eat. I wanted to try out my new attitude at night when there wasn't as much pedestrian traffic on the street. Once out of the building I stopped at my favorite street vendor, all the while looking for a tail. Again nothing unusual so I walked around for a couple of hours and finally back to my hotel.

I woke up earlier the next day and just for a lark I unscrewed the wall plates again and stood back in shock when I exposed another listening device in the same wall receptacle. I didn't even bother to remove this one. I just started talking out loud to my audience. It must have sounded a little strange, this one-way conversation but I was getting the message loud and clear. I would never be out of their sight and I would be just an asset to them. I was on the team but not an equal partner. I would have to carry out my orders to the letter and I would have to act in a professional manner at all times. I kept saying over and over in my mind and out loud that these guys were good. I then announced to my invisible audience that I was on my way to the park to play a game of chess and they could find me there if they so chose.

I left my room and walked to the park, not bothering to look around anymore, knowing full well I had company. I didn't bother to join in the usual crowd watching the most interesting match. Instead I found a hustler and sat down for a game of my own. The first match we played I couldn't really concentrate that well but I insisted on playing again and again. We played for several hours before I had had enough. The game took my mind off of the obvious and with no contact I decided to walk back to the hotel.

I was about to start back when I spotted Ariela enter the park. She joined one of the crowds and then, glancing over in my direction, indicated for me to join her. I stood up and walked over and said hello. She didn't answer, just turned away and began to walk out of the park and down the avenue. I followed at a safe distance. We walked for at least an hour until she came to a diner and went in and took a seat. I followed her into the place and sat down with her.

She had cleaned up considerably from the previous meeting and her striking beauty was showing through. It was amazing the transformation from the sleazy tramp to the lovely lady that was sitting across from me. We exchanged pleasantries and she asked if I had eaten, to which I replied sarcastically, "You tell me," and then I handed her the listening device I had removed from the wall receptacle in my room.

She was unmoved and suggested we order some breakfast before we talk. I hadn't eaten in too many restaurants since I had arrived, so I was going to take advantage of this occasion. I ordered a breakfast special and coffee and sat back taking in her beauty. The way she looked at me and her body language was telling me not to get any ideas but it was impossible. I wondered if they picked her for this mission for her competency or her looks.

After we ate she told me I was to check out of my hotel and travel by train up to Montreal. She then said she would meet me there with further instructions. She said we would have to decide upon a meeting place and asked me about Montreal.

"I've never been there before," I said, "and I don't speak a word of French." The only thing I knew about that city was what I had learned from watching "Hockey Night in Canada," a television sports show that was really Canada's national identity. "Let's meet in front of the Montreal Forum." It was the only landmark I could think of. We agreed on a time and a date, left the restaurant and parted company, losing each other in the crowd almost immediately.

"Well," I said out loud, "I wonder who will be with me on the train?" I didn't waste any time. I walked to Penn Station, the terminal for trains destined for Canada. I checked the schedule and booked a reservation on the next morning's train to Montreal.

I walked back to my hotel, stretched out on the bed, and said out loud, "Oh, what the hell," and got up and unscrewed the wall plate covering the listening device and saw it had been removed. These guys are all over me, I thought. I was determined to expose whoever would be with me on the train ride north.

The next day I was awake earlier than I had been for a month. My only luggage was a backpack and it was half empty. I checked out of the hotel that had been my home for over a month and began my walk to the station.

It began to occur to me that what I was doing was a very serious criminal offence. I was in the employ of a foreign country on a mission to assassinate two third country nationals in the country of my birth. I began to realize that it was true what Ben told me while he held a loaded pistol at my throat. I was nothing more than a hired killer, a mercenary. It had also been true when I shouldered arms for the United States in a conflict that had nothing to do with me. And now it was the only thing that defined me. I began to wonder what my role in this thing could be if these people could move around like ghosts. They had been in my hotel room at will. Every minute of every day they could account for my whereabouts without the least bit of suspicion on my part. I was eager to find out what they could possibly need me for.

CHAPTER NINE

I reached the station in plenty of time and began to wander around. As at most transportation hubs in the United States, there were lots of GI's on leave and I fit right in with them. We talked and laughed and I hooked up with a kid on his way to a little town in upstate New York. He was on his first trip home after returning from Vietnam and he looked nervous and uptight.

We talked about the difference during my time and his. I had been back for a few years and the fighting was still going on. He had been a door gunner on a medivac helicopter and he told me that his mission was flying the ARVNs around. Like most people in America he was sick of the thought of Southeast Asia and just wanted to talk about girls and how everything was going to be perfect now that he was going home. I remembered how I had had a similar kind of attitude when I got back but somehow things seemed to change. I lost myself in booze and drugs, wanting to scream out what I had been through to people who were more interested in the football score.

He was shocked when he realized I was a Canadian and had volunteered, whereas he was drafted and had no interest in anything military. "I wish I would have known you before and you could have taken my place," he said as we took our seats and the train began to pull out of the station. I thought, if you just knew what else I had volunteered for you would think I am really crazy. I began spinning a lie to him about having a job in New York and was just going home for the weekend. Being a liar was new to me but he appeared to believe me so I kept it up. It struck me that everything from now on was going to be a lie so I better get good at it.

The train trip was magnificent. We traveled along the Hudson River with a superb view of places like West Point Military Academy. My companion had been on this trip many times and acted as a kind of tour guide. It was obvious that even though he was sick of killing and war he had that patriotic fervor that first struck me about the American boys I had met in boot camp. I don't ever remember anything like that in Canada. In Canada we seemed to get our fill of that stuff on television and left the reality of it to the Americans. My traveling buddy was going home to a little town on the western shore of Lake Champlain called Westport. His family had lived there for hundreds of years and his father owned the pharmacy. He intended to go into business with his father when he got out of the service and would have been headed in that direction already if he hadn't been drafted right out of college. Now that his service was up he wouldn't be looking back.

For me it was just the opposite. I had no education and had nothing to return to and where I was going and what I was doing was anybody's guess.

When he got off at his stop there must have been a hundred people to greet him. I got a little teary-eyed myself when I saw him embracing his mother and father on the train platform. It was a scene out of Norman Rockwell. The great American spirit. It made me think of what I had become; there would never be a homecoming like that for me. I was traveling down a much different road. It was like this was my destiny and that was his. He also had a girl waiting for him; I couldn't see her in the crowd but I'm sure she was there. As the train pulled out of the station he never looked back at it. He would take off his uniform and carry on where he left off before he got drafted and I would remain behind on the train heading north, looking for a victim.

It was early in the evening when the train pulled into the station in Montreal. I felt that I was in a foreign county when I walked out of the station and heard the people speaking French. I had been forced to take French classes back in high school but I was always the class fool and made fun of the teacher and the language and subsequently failed the course. I probably could have been the best student if I had employed my father's strict discipline. I proved that by being able to memorize Shakespeare and operas in Italian but failed to be able to apply myself in school. I was always in trouble and the words of the officer back in Tel Aviv came to me. He said I had a personality defect and when he said it I became really pissed. Now walking out of the station and into the huge square that greeted me I began to hear my teachers as they would regularly scold me. To make matters worse I could see the outlines of a huge cathedral at the opposite end of the square and it took me back to the nuns and my escapades in the Catholic school.

My first impression of Montreal was that I was going to hate the place and I wanted to get the job over with as soon as possible and get the hell out of there. I thought that coming back to Canada I would feel something, like this was my home, but I felt just the opposite. I really felt lost and it only got worse when I was ignored when I asked for directions to a cheap hotel. I finally found someone who would speak to me in English and I was directed to a hotel in the old part of the city near Chinatown. I took a taxi from Dominion Square to Rue Saint Dominique and was dropped off in front of a hotel. It was a warm summer evening and there were lots of people on the street but not anything like New York. Once inside the hotel I was relieved to learn that the desk clerk spoke English and they had a vacancy. After securing a place to stay for the next week I made my way to my room and once inside I quickly fell asleep.

The next morning I asked at the front desk for directions to the Forum and was happy to learn I could walk there. It was also located in old Montreal, on the corner of Atwater Avenue and Sainte Catherine Street. I was pointed in the right direction and left on my way. My meeting with Ariela was scheduled for that morning in front of this old landmark. I had heard the name of this place many times while watching hockey games on our old black and white television but never dreamed I would actually be standing in front of this monument to Canadian history. I was about to make a little Canadian history myself, I thought.

I found the building with little trouble and began to pace back and forth in front of it. I may have received some training back in Tel Aviv but I wasn't trained how to be inconspicuous. I must have looked like I was waiting for my first job interview. I paced back and forth for over an hour when a dark-colored sedan with diplomatic license plates pulled up to the curb. A man got out and motioned me to join him. When I walked over to the car he unceremoniously ushered me into the back seat between him and another man and the car sped off into the morning traffic.

In the car were four members of the team with my old friend Ben behind the wheel. He immediately took control of the situation. There was no back slapping or nice to see you pleasantries, it was right down to business.

"Where's Ariela"? I asked.

Ben replied sarcastically, "You like Ariela?"

"No," I said, "I was just wondering. She said she was going to meet me here."

"Never mind about her," he said. I could see by the way Ben was taking charge that he was going to be the team leader and I was going to have to suck it up. I was used to taking orders from all kinds of people up the chain of command starting with Staff Sergeant Mejia so this was not going to be any different. I already hated this guy but I had the utmost respect for him also. I was also fully aware he wouldn't hesitate to kill me if he had good reason and he knew that I was capable of the same. I couldn't remember the names of the other three agents in the car and they didn't say a word. The agent to my left had a file folder in his hand and while Ben was talking he opened it.

"You see this vehicle?" Ben said. I could see a pickup truck with a camper set up on the back. This type of recreational vehicle was common all over Canada. Families used them for all kinds of outdoor activities, from hunting and fishing vacations to cross-country travel. "I want you to find one of these vehicles," he said. "It must be used but reliable, have Quebec license plates and insurance, and I want you to purchase it. I also want you to start looking for an apartment or a house to rent in the Blainville area."

Ben went on to describe Blainville, Quebec. It was a small city that had lots of tourist activity. The city was located at the foot of what was referred to as the Canadian Shield where there was a ski hill and it was also perfect for accessing Autoroute 15, which he said we would be using a lot. I was then handed an envelope full of money and a piece of paper with the picture of the truck and the name Blainville scribbled across it. Ben drove like he did on the obstacle course where I had first met him and by the time we stopped I didn't have a clue where I was. He said before I was dropped off at the curb that we would meet at the same place, same time, in one week. He also told me to get myself some new clothes because I looked like a bum. I was left on the side of the road as the car sped off into the traffic.

In New York the people who hung out at the park were dressed very casually and, other than the thousands of students that passed through the park, I had thought I fit in quite well. I thought to myself, OK, I have an envelope full of money and I am going to find someplace to spend it. I had never owned a suit in my life and I was in the perfect place to buy one. I remembered back in Vietnam when a couple of marines came back from R&R in Hong Kong they had these tailor-made suits jammed into their sea bags and they would hang them up when we were in base camp. I wondered if they ever got a chance to wear them after they got home—if they got home.

I found my way back to Sainte Catherine Street and walked along until I found a menswear shop. When I entered the shop the first thing I noticed was that when it became obvious that I was there to spend some money the employees spoke perfect English. I enjoyed every minute in the store and came away with a whole new wardrobe. I took a taxi back to my hotel and tried on my new outfit in front of the mirror. I was amazed at how different I could feel with a spiffy set of duds on. I really started to imagine myself as a secret agent. That evening I dressed up and went out and ate a meal in a fancy restaurant. I even ordered a bottle of wine. I was a little tipsy when I left the restaurant and was feeling quite full of myself. I was beginning to go through a serious change and decided I was ready to play the part.

That night, lying in bed, it occurred to me that if this hit was going to take place back in New York they would never need me for anything. They were very well set up there, but showing up in an embassy car made them look vulnerable. I imagined that they must have driven down that morning from Ottawa where all the embassies were located. I then looked up at the ceiling and began to construct my chessboard. I hadn't resorted to this since my incarceration but now I had a reason: I was now in the chess game of my life. The big difference now was that I was neither white nor black, I was the third party and for the first time I felt powerful. I decided right then to make a bold opening. I thought back to the kibbutz and my first teacher when he said that "the chess opening will determine the course of the game." I opened with the king knight and fell asleep planning my next move.

I woke up with the intention of bringing up the business of my $20,000 when I saw Ben again. As far as I knew the money had yet to materialize in my bank account back in New York. With my newfound confidence I had a hop in my step that hadn't been there before. I walked out of the hotel that morning determined not to live on street vendor food any more. I found a nice restaurant with complimentary newspapers, sat down, and ordered breakfast. I flipped the pages over to the used car section and began to search for my first automobile. I had never purchased a vehicle before and didn't know what it entailed so I picked out the name of a used car dealership, ate breakfast, and went on the hunt.

Never in my wildest dream did I think that I would ever regret being the class fool when I was made to study French in high school but being in Montreal made me feel that way. The day before was one thing in the fancy menswear shop on Sainte Catherine Street. Today, after my first car dealership, I was really on the defensive. I supposed it was because I was so young and was asking about a recreational vehicle that the fast talking salesman thought I wasn't serious. He was in fact so rude to me that I thought I should just step to one side and give him a kick in the side of the head. It was all I could do to control myself. I walked from dealership to dealership before coming to one with a friendly, English-speaking old man who reminded me of my grandfather. I spun him a yarn about why I needed this vehicle and he was only too helpful. He didn't have one on his lot but if I was serious he said he would find just the vehicle I was looking for. I showed him the wad of bills I had in my pocket and he assured me I had come to the right place. He told me to come back the next day and he would have two or three different models on the lot for me to choose from. I walked off the lot whispering to myself, "Knight to bishop file three."

I enjoyed the walk back to the hotel and decided to check for any bugs that the team might have installed in my room. I had brought my screwdriver from New York and went to work going over the entire room. I removed all the wall plates and found nothing. I then loosened the light fixtures and came up empty. I looked everywhere I could think and couldn't find anything. I concluded that no one had been in my room except perhaps the chamber maid. I began to sense that New York was one thing but Montreal was another. In New York they were in and out of my room at will and up here in Canada they were driving around in a car with diplomatic license plates. It was starting to make sense to me now what my role in this nasty business was going to be.

The next morning I walked back to the car dealership and there on the lot were three different trucks that might be what I was looking for. The salesman met me beside one of the pickups, eager to make a sale to this young kid with a pocket full of money. In typical fashion the first vehicle that he showed me was old and ready to fall apart. Rust everywhere on the body, and inside the camper was dirty and smelly. He then quoted me the price and I was in shock. "For that piece of junk?" I groaned. "You must be kidding!"

I had never bought a car in my life but everyone was aware of the reputation of car salesmen and this nice old grandfather type was proving all the stories to be true. He showed me the other two trucks, which progressively got better and along the way more expensive. He then ushered me into his office for the final sales pitch. Business must have been poor that month because he never shut up. He was trying to convince me that I was getting a vehicle for free and his grandkids would be going hungry if I didn't buy one of his trucks.

We finally agreed on a price for one of the vehicles and I dug the cash out of my pockets. I noticed his eyes light up when I started piling the bills on his desk. I had an awkward time stacking and counting the bills, which he was only too eager to help with. I had never had any money in my life so it was a new experience for me to see what cash money could do to people. I could see how a stack of bills on a table had changed his personality so dramatically. I made a special note of this exchanging of bills and quietly said under my breath, "Queen pawn to fourth rank." He was very organized and had a girl from an agency drive out to the car lot and fix me up with registration and insurance. After I paid her in cash and took possession of the paperwork, I climbed into the cab of the truck, started the engine, and asked, "Which way to Blainville?"

I hadn't driven a vehicle for what seemed to be years but got the hang of it right away. I noticed that driving a pickup truck with a camper on the back meant the other cars on the road gave me a lot of room.

I was lost as soon as I left the car lot and found driving around Montreal not to be an easy task. I found out the city was located on an island and everywhere you went there were bridges to cross. I was aware that Manhattan was also an island but I never had a vehicle and never bothered to walk across any of the bridges there. I drove around for hours never locating Autoroute 15. I decided I would need to know how to get around in this city anyway so I kept driving around for hours. I was feeling quite smug about myself evolving from a pedestrian to a vehicle operator when the words of an old aunt of mine rang out in my head. She was a wise old lady who was always saying, "Put a peasant on a horse and he thinks he's a king." Now, for the first time since I first heard her repeat that line, I could understand what she meant.

I had a difficult time finding a parking spot in the old city of Montreal and was finally accepted in an overnight parking lot several miles from my hotel. I parked the truck and found it easier to negotiate my way back to my hotel on foot. Once back in my room I decided I would have to purchase a map of the area and draw out my route to Blainville. That would be tomorrow but on this night I was going to dress up in my fancy duds and go out for dinner again. I had quite enjoyed my meal the night before and decided there was no reason to pinch pennies anymore as I was on the job now.

The girl on the desk at the hotel helpfully provided me with a map, and drew out my route from the city to the Laurentian Mountains. She asked if I was a skier.

I said "Ya, I'm looking for a place for the winter." It had not occurred to me that I would need a story and she had just come up with one for me. I had become a natural at lying. It just flowed out of my mouth like I believed it.

Everything seemed to be going my way. I dressed up in my suit and walked over to the same restaurant I had eaten at the night before. Tonight I skipped the wine. I could tell from the night before if I had a weakness it was alcohol and I was starting to play a role I wasn't trained for and wasn't about to screw it up over a bottle of wine.

Walking back to my hotel after dinner in the warm summer evening I decided to check my room for bugs again to see if I was being shadowed as I had been in New York. I thought that they must have had someone staying in the same hotel as me and when I left, an agent had entered the room, placed the listening device, and was out in minutes. I also thought if that type of surveillance was all they had this mission could be compromised very easily. I removed all the wall receptacle covers in the room but found nothing and it bolstered my confidence.

The next morning, armed with my map and directions, I climbed into my pickup truck and headed out of the city of Montreal north on Autoroute 13. I crossed two bridges and took the off ramp to Autoroute 15 and I soon found myself in downtown Blainville. I expected nice countryside but other than the beginning of the great Canadian Shield mountain range it looked like a mini-industrial area. I stopped at a hotel restaurant and found myself in over my head. No one spoke

English here at all, and even ordering a meal was going to be difficult. Finally, after a few awkward moments a waitress with a modicum of heavily-accented English found her way to my table and took my order. While waiting for my meal, I bought a copy of the local paper. It was in French. I decided right then that unless I got some help with the language I was not going to be able to get anything done. I ate my meal, paid the waitress, and taking my French newspaper, I climbed into the cab of my truck and began the drive back to Montreal.

I missed the interchange that would take me back to the auto route and I ended up driving around Blainville for an hour. There were several hotels in the city and I decided to drive back to Montreal, check out of my hotel, and move into one up here. I noticed that there were large parking lots in front of the hotels here, and that alone was reason enough to leave the congestion and parking problems of Montreal behind me.

I drove back into the city, memorizing landmarks that I would need to make this drive easier. I parked the truck at the same overnight parking lot as the night before and made the long walk back to my hotel.

When it was time for dinner I dressed up in my new suit and made my way back to my restaurant. I was really getting to like eating there. The waiters were friendly and spoke English. It was also close to the hotel and they must have gotten a lot of business from there. I had never in my life left a tip anywhere for anything but noticed it was the thing to do and followed suit. I began to lose myself in the lifestyle surrounded by seemingly normal people. It struck me that I was no more than a paid assassin in their midst but fit in just the same. I was beginning to see what kind of an asset I could be. I looked young and green, a typical Canadian from western Canada—anything but a Middle Eastern assassin.

In the morning I checked out of the hotel, walked back to where the truck was parked, paid the attendant, and drove out of the city. I had no trouble finding my way to the country this time and decided I wouldn't ask the team for help with an interpreter. The team probably wanted it that way. I knew that I stuck out like a sore thumb no matter what measures I took to fit in with the locals but at least I could muster up a story. The same could not be said for the rest of the team, with heavy Israeli accents and Middle Eastern looks.

I arrived in Blainville and parked in the lot of a very large hotel. It had a grand front entrance, with the rooms off to the sides like giant wings. It also had a huge parking lot where I could park the truck without it being noticed by anyone.

I picked up a copy of the local newspaper and walked into the hotel lobby and through the doors into the restaurant, sat down, and ordered breakfast. I was in luck this morning and was served by a nice young lady who spoke passable English. Since the breakfast rush was obviously over I asked her if she could help me with the newspaper, which she was happy to do. It being the off season for cross-country skiing in the area there were several houses for lease and I arranged for her to help me with the language problem after work.

With nothing else to do I walked out to the truck and opened up the back door and climbed in. I could see now why the team wanted a vehicle like this. It was spacious with a place to cook, a bed to sleep in, and lots of windows to sneak a look out of. And I had noticed trucks very similar to this one on the roads everywhere I drove. There were even a couple that looked similar in the same parking lot. It was so unnoticeable it might as well have been invisible.

The waitress was on the early shift so I didn't have to wait all day. Before long she came walking out from a side door in the hotel. I met her in the parking lot and we walked back into the lobby of the hotel to use the telephone. She looked over the paper and began phoning the numbers listed and then began to interpret for me. By now I was beginning to become a pretty good liar and cooked up a story about my family wanting to move up here and go cross-country skiing this winter and we needed a furnished house. With that information she had a story to tell the landlord and the only word that I could make out in the whole conversation was "l'Anglay." It sounded like "the English" and she had to do a lot of talking when that word came up.

When she got off the phone she told me that there was an old farmhouse for rent a few kilometers from town and we could go out and view the place right then. She said she would come along and interpret for me and I agreed to pay her for her time. We drove out of Blainville north toward the Laurentian Mountains for about fifteen minutes before coming to a turn-off that soon turned into a gravel road, and then we turned off into a driveway.

There it was, a cute old French Canadian farmhouse that must have been standing for a hundred years. The owner was waiting for us in front of the house, a little old man who looked as old as the house. He showed us all around outside and inside. In the meantime the two of them never stopped talking and I couldn't understand a word they were saying. When the tour was over we agreed on a price and I leased a home for a year. I didn't really think a year was necessary but I was going to take what I could get. I gave the old man a cash deposit and agreed to return the next day to sign the lease.

We drove back into Blainville and I dropped my interpreter off on a street corner. I thanked her profusely and overpaid her. I was quite pleased at how well things had gone so far and was feeling that I would have some real progress to report to my superiors in a couple of days. As I drove back toward Montreal I said out loud, "Queen bishop to fourth rank." I had by this time forgotten which chess opening I was talking about. I was just full of myself thinking I was some kind of secret agent.

I drove back to Montreal in the pickup truck, parked it in the overnight parking lot, and walked back to the hotel. That evening I again dressed up in my new suit of clothes and went out to eat at my restaurant. I knew I shouldn't but I ordered a bottle of wine anyway and proceed to get a little loose. I could get used to this very easily, I thought, as I was being served by the waiters. I made a point of enjoying myself that evening knowing I would be chopping wood and building a fire in an old wood stove the next night if I was to have a meal.

After the initial sense of well-being, the wine made me a little paranoid. When I left the restaurant and walked back to the hotel I was careful to look and listen for a tail, but couldn't spot anyone. When I got back to my hotel I even checked for bugs in the wall receptacles and found none.

The next morning I checked out of the hotel, my only luggage being my backpack and my new suit. What a contrast, I thought as I walked down the street, a backpack and a fancy suit; there really is no in-between in my life.

I drove out of the city, over the bridges, and into the country. It was a beautiful summer day and I was looking forward to some country living.

When I reached the farmhouse I parked the truck and moved in bag and baggage. There were several things I hadn't counted on once I began to look around the place. It was still summertime but I could see that the only heat was the wood stove in the kitchen and the fireplace. I thought it would be an adventure cooking over a wood stove and thought chopping wood could be fun but was starting to realize what all the talking had been about the previous day. The old farmer must have been telling my interpreter that I didn't know what I was getting myself into.

There was an ancient refrigerator in the house that seemed to be in working order so I drove into Blainville looking for a grocery store. Grocery shopping was a new experience for me and I wondered out loud what cooking was going to be like never having cooked anything before but a hamburger.

I purchased a few staples and drove back to the farmhouse, a little anxious about cooking on a wood stove but willing to give it a try. Once back at the farmhouse I found an axe in an almost empty woodshed and gathered up enough kindling to make a fire in the kitchen stove. With sweat dripping down my forehead I cooked up a hamburger and enjoyed my first meal out in the country.

The next few days were as close to heaven as I had ever known. I puttered about the place and learned a lot about how to cook over a wood stove. It just wasn't like turning on the gas in a modern kitchen. There were electric lights and an indoor bathroom which I was thankful for, and I had several long, hot soaks in the old-fashioned tub.

A week soon passed and I was up early on the morning of my next meet in Montreal. I drove into the city as though I was a resident. I was able to pick out landmarks that I hadn't noticed on the previous drives down Autoroute 15. Once on Montreal Island I found a place to park and walked to the front of the Forum where I had met my handlers the week before. I was only there for a few minutes when what looked like the same car that I had met the week before pulled up and I jumped in.

The seating arrangements were the same as the previous week. I was ushered in between the two agents in the back seat. And Ben, who was doing the driving, began to question me as though I was a criminal.

I was quite proud of my accomplishments and was told to draw a map to the farmhouse. Ben then asked me to hand over the keys to the truck and at the same time I was handed another envelope full of money and instructed to go and buy another vehicle. This time it was to be a car much like the one that we were traveling in.

I directed them to where I had parked the truck, handed the keys to one of the agents, and watched him drive off. I was then told to get out of the car, go and buy the other vehicle, and they would see me at the farmhouse. They left me standing at the side of the road.

One minute I was feeling on top of the world and the next I was in the depths of depression. I stood on the side of the street not knowing where I was or which way to go. I thought it was amazing how alone these people could make me feel. I was convinced I was doing a good job, and then they came by and made me feel worthless.

I decided to find my way to the used car lot where I had purchased the pickup truck. I might as well go back to the same old man, I thought, since he had made it so easy. I began to walk in what I thought was the right direction, thinking I would have to come up with a story for the old guy. I was getting to like spending all this money and as long as there seemed to be an endless supply I decided I was going to enjoy myself. I had to walk several miles and by the time I got to the car lot I had a weak but plausible story for the old man.

When I walked up to his office he gave me a strange look. We exchanged pleasantries but it seemed to me that he had the look of someone who just got caught stealing something. "So, how's the truck running?" he asked in a sheepish way.

The way he asked the question I could see he was waiting for me to tell him that the truck fell apart and I wanted my money back. "I got drunk and hit a pole," I answered. "The truck is a write-off." I could see a sigh of relief come over his face.

"Did you get yourself a DUI?" he asked, trying to make conversation.

"No," I said. "I made it home before the cops showed up."

"You didn't get hurt, did you?" he asked, sizing me up.

"No, I'm fine," I replied.

"So you'll be looking for another truck?" he asked.

"No, I'm looking for a car this time," I said.

His demeanor changed in an instant. "Well, son," he said, "you have come to the right place." He hopped up from behind his desk and led me out of the door to the lot. He then went into his well-rehearsed sales pitch. "How much are you wanting to spend today?" he asked as we walked toward the high-end vehicles. I in turn dodged the question and started asking the prices of the nondescript four-door sedans like the one that had just unceremoniously left me on the side of the road.

We found one that looked like a family vehicle and I took it for a test drive. I was getting a little more worldly now. I hadn't even bothered to take the truck for a test drive before I bought it and perhaps that is why he was not so surprised to see me. I liked the first car I tried and we settled on a price, and the same as before he called the insurance girl and I drove out of the lot in my new set of wheels. "Queen knight to fourth rank," I said to myself as I wheeled toward Autoroute 15.

I drove straight back to the farmhouse, only stopping in Blainville to buy some groceries. After only a few days the place was starting to feel like home and I almost forgot why I was even there.

Two days later, Ben, accompanied by a woman, drove my old truck down the driveway and into the yard. When they got out and walked into the house I was pleasantly surprised to welcome Ariela into my house. Ben, on the other hand, was still an asshole as far as I was concerned but I gathered by now that he was the team captain and I would have to follow his orders to the letter. He in turn would have to play his role to perfection if we were going to pull this off. It was also beginning to dawn on me that if anything went wrong there was only going to be one patsy and that would be me.

I made some coffee while they began to pack some suitcases into the house. Then over coffee Ben told me that we would have to go into Montreal the next day to purchase another car and start looking for an apartment in West Island. He went on to explain that West Island was the English-speaking section of Montreal and we would require an apartment there for more members of the team. He also told me that our hunt had not begun in earnest yet but intelligence had assured him that our targets were still in this area. I felt like a dummy when I had been struggling with the French language everyday and I could have been in an English-speaking area all the time. I mentioned that to him but he said, "We will need more cars and apartments next week and it won't just be in West Island."

It was going to be awkward the first day with the three of us in the house and I was sent into Blainville to purchase some sleeping bags and pillows. When I returned Ariela had the kitchen smelling wonderful and Ben had the only table in the house covered with all kinds of electronic devices, some looking curiously familiar to the one I had removed from my room in New York. I sat back and let the two of them take over the place and I especially watched Ben as closely as I could, asking him questions until he got pissed off at me and sent me outside to chop some wood.

Next, Ben ordered me to drive into Blainville to the telephone company to get a telephone hooked up. Before I left, Ariela handed me a shopping list. I began see that my role now in this mission was schlepping stuff around for these professionals and staying out of their way.

I drove into Blainville and found the telephone company and in the fashion I was beginning to become accustomed to struggled to find someone who spoke English. I accomplished my mission and drove back to the farm with my groceries and receipt for the telephone hookup.

We ate a meal that afternoon as a kind of family. I was amazed at how Ariela could change like a chameleon. She was able to look like a soldier in uniform or a whore on the streets of New York or now, in this setting, a farm girl organizing a farm kitchen. I wasn't about to be fooled by this little show of domesticity, however. She was probably a killer just like me. It also occurred to me that if she was given the order she would terminate my contract in an instant.

We didn't discuss much about the mission, just the fact that Ben and I were going to travel into Montreal the next day and I was to purchase another car. He liked the one I had already bought and wanted another one that looked similar but a different color. As for sleeping arrangements, I was moved out of the bedroom and slept on a couch in the living room while Ben slept in the camper.

The next day Ben and I made the trip into Montreal, Ben doing the driving as always. When we arrived in the city he asked me where I wanted to go to purchase the next vehicle. I had to think if I really wanted to go back to the same place. It was easy to deal with the old man who spoke English but he was sure to grow suspicious of me. I decided what the hell, I would come up with some kind of story, and after Ben produced another envelope full of cash I had him drop me off near the car dealership.

I walked onto the lot trying to come up with a plausible story when the old man noticed me and walked out of the office. He greeted me like an old friend but the look on his face told me that any story I came up with would not do and that I would be better off waiting for him to start the conversation.

"Have another car wreck?" he asked in a sly manner.

"Ya, something like that," was the best I could come with, and he asked me if I was looking for another vehicle. I then came up with a good one and told him that my brother liked the car so much that I sold it to him.

It was obvious that he knew I was lying and said I should get a job selling cars. Then he looked straight at me and said, "Look, kid, I know you're up to something but if you want another car I'll sell it to you no questions asked."

"That will be fine with me," I replied.

Because I didn't know anything about Montreal and never read the papers I didn't realize that I was in the bank robbery capital of North America and it was the old man's suspicion that I was involved in something along those lines. We picked out a similar car in a different color and without dickering over the price we went through the now familiar paperwork process and I drove off the lot. I knew he was taking advantage of me with the price and this must have confirmed to him that I was some kind of a crook with wads of cash. He in turn must have been in the used-car business long enough to have seen about everything there is to see and he fit the profile of the shady used-car salesman to a tee. Before driving away I told the old man I would be back and he gave me a wink.

I drove out of Montreal over the bridge and out into the country thinking, "Black king pawn to fourth rank."

I arrived back at the farm with my new car and was soon ordered, this time by Ariela, to get busy chopping wood and when that was finished to drive into Blainville and arrange for someone to drop off a load of firewood for the winter. That order confirmed that this mission might take a long time and we might be here all winter. I told her that there were probably ads for firewood for sale in the paper but it was all in French.

"Go get a paper," she said. "French is my fourth language."

"Jeez, thanks for telling me," I said.

I got the proverbial reply, "Well, you never asked."

Never asked, I said to myself, well, that won't happen again.

I went to Blainville, got the paper, and after studying it for some time, Ariela happily informed me that when the telephone was working she would order the firewood.

Ben was in the kitchen when I returned, working on his electronic gadgets. He told me that I was to travel back into Montreal the next day and start looking for an apartment in the English-speaking part of the city. He instructed me as to the specifics and general area. I immediately saw this as one of my easiest tasks so far because now I knew that there was an English language newspaper available with a rental section. I was confident that I would be able to find an apartment without any trouble. I also asked him about my money that was supposed to be in my bank account in New York and he told me not to worry, that the money was there. "You are going to New York in a week and can see for yourself."

We ate dinner like a little family again. I noticed that they never spoke one word of Hebrew and thought that it wasn't out of politeness to me. It must have been a standing order. Right then I wondered how the other team had got it so wrong in Lillehammer if these people were so efficient, and then it dawned on me, that's where I came in. All the training in the world could not make up for what I was providing. Everything was in my name. If they left today it would be like they had never been here, but my footprints were everywhere. I remembered the spy novel I read in New York where, when one of the agents outlived his usefulness, they just eliminated him. It was at that moment that I decided that if that was the plan for me I was going to find some way to cover my back but just how I didn't know. In the meantime I also noticed that we were going to have a lot of time on our hands, so I decided to buy a chessboard and see if anyone could play chess.

There was a little black and white television with one French channel that the two of them obviously understood and we all watched it for a while before assuming the same sleeping arrangements and turning in for the night.

The next day it was back on the road and into Montreal. I was getting very familiar with the ride, and Ben instructed me to drive around the city and become familiar with as much of the area as possible. I drove to the English-speaking area of the city and bought a newspaper. There were so many apartments for rent that I decided I should drive back to the farm and get some advice as to which one to view. I did spend the rest of the day driving around the city, getting to know the street names that were mostly in French. I only interrupted my drive to stop to get something to eat and to buy a chess set and a "how to play chess" book. All the driving and trying to remember French names made me dizzy so after a while I drove back to the farm.

Ariela and Ben were both gone when I arrived so I just settled in and started reading the paper from front to back. When I got to the entertainment section I noticed an ad for auditions for a Shakespeare play. "Wow," I said, and it had to be "Othello." An English play in Montreal, I thought, I wonder if they will get an audience. I decided that if I was still around when it opened I would go to see it. I had never actually been to a performance of the play but still knew it word for word from my father's inculcations when I was a child.

When Ben and Ariela returned I already had the fire lit in the stove and had the chess set out trying out some openings. I immediately cleared the table, packing up the board and pieces along with my book.

Ben was all business and asked how my apartment hunting was going and I explained that I wanted his advice on which places I should ask to view.

After dinner I got out the newspaper and with a pencil we carefully went over each ad, crossing out the ones that didn't fit our criteria and underlining several that did.

In an off-hand manner I mentioned the Shakespeare play auditions and then in an out of character manner I went on to tell the two of them about my childhood and how I was very familiar with the play "Othello." Ben sat back and in an angry tone barked out, "Shakespeare was an anti-Semitic bigot and I would never go to one of his plays." Ariela concurred with him and the two of them voiced their disgust for the English playwright.

I was sorry I had mentioned it and tried to change the subject, getting back to the vacancy ads when Ben's tone changed. His sense of the mission and his extensive training took over. He was trained to use every means at his disposal. I could see he was thinking hard and then he spoke. "You are going to audition for the play."

I looked at him and laughed. "You're kidding, right?"

"No, if you are telling the truth about your vast knowledge of this particular play, you should be able to win a part."

"But I'm not an actor," I said.

"What do think you have been doing for the past six months but acting?" he said.

"But on a stage?" I said. "I don't think I could do it."

"That's the end of it," he said. "I am ordering you to attend the auditions and win a part in that play."

He then went on, "You are not the secret in this operation, we are. I want you out in the public where you can be seen and heard. What better way than in a play? You need a reason to be around and now you have one. When you get back from New York you will attend the auditions and that's final."

While trying to get to sleep that night, thoughts kept going around in my head. I hadn't thought about my family in a long time; in fact, we were almost estranged but that really wasn't the case. I was just not the family type. And the words of the officer back in Tel Aviv went over and over in my head, how he determined that I was a little bit off the beam. I had one of the most difficult nights of my life on the couch that night, but it had nothing to do with my physical discomfort. Notwithstanding that, I would have liked to crawl into bed with Ariela. I was convinced that she would slit my throat if I tried but it was the one thought that helped me to finally fall asleep.

The next day it was back on the road and into Montreal. I found a phone booth and started telephoning the numbers in the ads we had underlined the night before. When I received a positive response I drove to my first viewing. Ben had coached me on the particular criteria we needed for this residence. He instructed me about the view, the parking, the building entrance and exits, the lane exits and entrances, and how easy it would be to merge with a decent flow of traffic. There could be no compromises with this location. The farm was one thing; it would be our general staging area but now with this apartment we were starting to close the noose and it was my job to make sure our location was perfect. In total I looked at four places that day, made extensive notes each time, and then drove back to the farm to make my report.

That evening we all went over my notes, and Ben decided that he and Ariela would follow me the next day and drive around each apartment building and then decide if any of these would fit into our plans.

Then I produced the chessboard and actually got Ben to engage me in a game of chess. He wasn't a great player but he was cunning. When I was in the middle of one of my moves he asked me to quote some Othello. From that one utterance I saw in him something that the game of chess was teaching me. I could also see Ben would do anything to win, and I liked that. He knew how to think many moves ahead and he was a good strategist. He was testing me to see how easily I could be thrown off my game. It was becoming obvious why he was tagged as the team leader. He was brimming with confidence and probably fearless and never stopped thinking. But I doubted he had as many notches on his pistol as I had and I intended to call him on it one day. I was also starting to like him a little bit even though the little matter of the scar on my chin screamed out for revenge.

I had to show him I was nonplussed about his request and began to run down the circumstances surrounding Othello, the Moor of Venice. It was extremely difficult to concentrate on the game at hand and describe the play at the same time but I was so familiar with all the aspects of it and I wanted to show Ben that I was up to the challenge. My father had made all of us children play all the parts in the play over and over again. I was sure that with a little prompting I could still remember the vast majority of all the parts. Two of the parts were daunting, namely the two lead parts, good and evil, represented by Othello himself and his lieutenant, Iago. When I started running down the outline I didn't proceed too far knowing it would instantly bore them and because a flood of emotions came over me. It didn't take me long to realize that my understanding of the play was through a child's eyes and I would need to buy a copy of the play and go over it.

I whipped Ben at chess that night with or without the distractions but gave him full marks for his display of cunning. I was, however, bothered by the thoughts that the play had dug up in my mind. The more I thought about the play the more my childhood came to mind. I had a difficult time falling asleep that night going over and over all the trouble I had got into as a child and then as a young man. Not to mention the fact that I was developing a romantic crush for Ariela that wasn't reciprocated in the least. She was sleeping soundly in the bedroom while I tossed and turned on the couch.

We took two cars into Montreal the next morning, stopping for breakfast at a restaurant and making out our plans for the day. I used the restaurant payphone to call three different numbers and made appointments that day to view the suites. Ben and Ariela would be cruising each neighborhood while I was in the suite with the landlord and then we would meet up afterwards and go over our notes.

By the end of the day I had been interviewed by the different landlords and my story had been tested to its limits. I drove back to the farmhouse totally exhausted.

That night after dinner we all went over our notes and decided on one two-bedroom furnished apartment that was located within walking distance of the theatre where "Othello" was to be performed. The play had become a big part of my story and I said to Ben that night, "What if I don't win a part?"

He replied matter-of-factly, "I'll see to it that you do."

The question seemed to throw him off a bit and I could see the cold look in his eyes. I instantly believed him and began to think how an unsuspecting thespian group would feel if they knew they were going up against Mossad for a part in an amateur production of Shakespeare. I decided right then I better buy a book of Shakespeare plays as soon as possible and brush up on my lines. I knew now it was a forgone conclusion that I would be in the play no matter what it took.

Ben handed an envelope of money to me the next morning and sent me into Montreal. I met with the landlord and signed a lease and paid him for the first and last months rent. He had had actors stay with him before so the story was totally believable and being a two bedroom he thought the place would be full of actors and artists. I drove back to the farm with my signed lease and the keys to my new apartment.

Things up to this point had not been all that serious but they were about to change. That night at our meeting Ben informed me that I was going to be taking a trip down south, first to New York to pick up some money, and then to rural America to purchase some firearms. It was almost hunting season and gun shows were starting to take place in many rural communities. He told me Ariela would meet me in New York after a flight from Ottawa and I would drive. He said he didn't want me to take too much money across the border because if I was stopped and had to undergo a search I had to come up clean.

Great, I thought. I'll have a chance to check my bank account and see if my money has been deposited. I could tell it was not a subject that Ben liked to talk about. I was sure he received a lousy civil service paycheck and the kind of money that I had been promised he couldn't save in a lifetime.

CHAPTER TEN

In preparation for my trip south to New York, Ben made a list of the firearms he wanted me to buy. It was detailed and included a number of .22 rimfire revolvers with speed loaders for offensive in-close work. He explained to me that although the revolvers were certainly more reliable we would also require heavier firepower for any defensive situations we might encounter. He gave me a wish list with the Beretta M951 being the most preferred because at the time it was standard issue with the Israeli Defense Force. Failing that I had others to look for, such as the Browning .380 and several Colt model .45's. The ammunition was as important as the weapons. In Canada everything was restricted, he said. We could find .22 caliber shells but anything like 9mm or .45 was impossible. He impressed on me the fact that there was no alternative to this mission. All our guns and ammo had to come from the U.S. and I should have no trouble filling out the list.

I was to rendezvous with Ariela at the same location in New York the next day and then head out into rural America. He said I would probably have more luck heading into the southern states where the gun shows were mostly unregulated

and a driver's license would be all the identification I would
need to make a purchase. Failing that, I still had my military
ID, which was better than a Canadian driver's license would
ever be.

I drove out of the farm onto Autoroute 15 and south
through Montreal to the Canada-United States border. It was
only about an hour and a half and at customs I was just waved
right through. On the other side of the border the auto route
connected with Interstate 87 and before I knew it I was driving
past Westport where I had witnessed the hero's homecoming
just a couple months before. I wondered as I left Westport and
Lake Champlain in my rearview mirror if I would ever receive
that kind of welcome anywhere.

The drive to New York City took all day and when I arrived
I was in the Bronx and as lost as I could be. I was in this
huge city with a car and that was one thing I had never ever
given any consideration to. Walking around Manhattan was
one thing but in this traffic I was going crazy. After driving
around for several hours I finally found an overnight parking
lot and pulled in and paid the attendant to park the car for
the night. It had never occurred to me that the car would be
such a hassle.

I took a taxi to the hotel I had stayed at the last time I
was in New York and got a room for the night. Before I went
upstairs I walked across the street to my favorite street vendor
and had my usual. He welcomed me back and we small talked
for a while; he and a few chess hustlers were the only people I
knew in the city. I made a joke to myself as I lay down on the
bed and spoke out loud that I didn't have my screwdriver or I
would have opened up the wall receptacles out of habit, and
fell asleep.

The next morning I made my usual trip across Manhattan
to the bank that had been the focus of my disappointment
every day for over a month. I waited in the usual line-up that
always took over an hour, and when it was my turn to ask the
teller as to the status of my account she responded with a

"mister" in front of my name. I had never seen so many zeros in my life. I thanked her and walked out of the bank with a hop in my step. Another couple of months and I will double that figure, I thought, but first back to work.

I spotted Ariela sitting in the park when I walked into the chess circle. There was the usual group of people standing around and everywhere chess matches were underway. It felt a little like home to me. I sat down beside her. She hadn't bothered to dress up in the costume she had worn the first time I had seen her here in Washington Square Park and our meeting didn't last more than a minute or so. I had a few questions for her and asked her what I was to do with the merchandise once I had acquired it. She told me that I was to meet her here in exactly two weeks with the list filled out. She then handed me an envelope just as before and stood up and walked away.

I hung around the park for a while looking in on a couple of chess matches that were underway before hailing a New York taxi cab. We traveled over the bridge in the direction of where I had stored the car and I began to think that I had no idea where to start looking for my first gun show when it dawned on me that if anyone knew where to buy guns it would be Morgan, my old Marine Corps buddy.

I had not bothered to even write to him since I had left college and climbed aboard the bus almost a year ago. I remembered him standing there waving to me as the bus drove off. By the look in his eyes I could tell he felt I was throwing my life away along with my one chance to take advantage of my veteran's benefits. He had kept me up most of the night trying to talk me out of dropping out of college and going up to New York and getting on that airplane. He just could not believe I would do something so stupid and he told me he was so tired of losing so many friends and that he just knew he would never see me again.

Morgan and his family were rooted in West Virginian history and he was truly at home whereas I was an itinerant and too easily influenced. In the end all of his urging had been of no use and I had left on that cool October morning. Now I was to return with an unbelievable story.

I somehow found my way onto Interstate 78 heading out of the city through New Jersey and towards Pennsylvania. Every time I stopped for gas I would ask directions until I was too tired to go any farther and stopped at a highway motel not far from Pittsburgh. That night for the first time as I lay in bed I went over the past year in my mind. How would I tell Morgan what I had got myself into? We were both killers but for him it was his patriotic duty and a long standing family tradition. It made me think of the first time I met Ben and he had showed his disgust for me. I rubbed my chin and felt the scar that his gun had left and finally fell asleep with his words going over in my head.

The next day I drove the rest of the way into West Virginia, curiously feeling at home in the Appalachian hills. From the interstate I proceeded on to the country road that I recognized and finally I turned on to the dirt road that led up the "holler" where Morgan's family had lived for a couple hundred years. It was so close to exactly a year since I had left even the color of the leaves on the trees looked the same.

Morgan's mother met me at the door and greeted me like a son. We sat on the porch swing and talked for hours. She filled me up with her finest cornbread and coffee and told me everything about every relative she had in the area. She was so proud of her son Morgan who had gone through a religious conversion in the past year and was actually doing some preaching at a little Baptist church over in Calhoun County. He was still going to college and was attending class at that moment. She also told me that Morgan had met a girl and was hoping that they would get married. She didn't ask me too many questions; having gone through a year of worry for her son while he served overseas she only wanted to look on the positive.

When Morgan drove into the yard I could see him through the window looking at my Quebec license tags and then running toward the house. He obviously thought it was me and that I must have made it back safely. He had served a full tour as a line grunt and lost many good friends and for him I was like a ghost coming back to life. When he came into the house he gave me a big hug and his eyes filled up with tears. "You made it," he said over and over. "I just can't believe it."

Morgan's mom went to work fixing a meal for a returning hero and we went out to feed his hounds and have a talk. Unlike his mother he wanted to know everything and I began telling him my tale. He had seen so many of his friends go crazy he didn't judge me a bit. He just sat and listened, asking a question here and there when something wasn't clear. At the end of my story all he could say in his slow distinctive West Virginia drawl was, "I always knew you was a crazy fucker, Kanook, but don't that beat everything."

When I was through talking he told me about his year and how he had assimilated back into country life without too many problems. He was bothered with nightmares like everyone but his faith had kept him strong. He invited me to see him preach at his church, Mt. Liberty Baptist, the next Sunday. He was also in love and insisted that I meet his girl. He had met her at college and he told me, "She's just the purdiest thang you ever saw." He said he wished that I would just stick around and go back to school but knew I was on a different course and nothing could stop me now. Morgan's mom had invited as many of their relatives as could show up for dinner and we had a country feast. These were real people, the backbone of America, patriotic, Bible-thumping Christians who also liked to have a good time.

Late that evening, after all of his relatives went home, Morgan and I sat out on the porch swing and began to talk. When we were in the corps and overseas there was never a better marine in the whole company. Morgan was fearless, he volunteered to walk point more than anyone in the platoon, and everyone thought he had a charm. I remembered my first day in the bush when he threatened to kill me if I didn't pull my weight. I was sure then that he would have and it was probably the best thing that could have happened to me. He hated any slackers and wasn't backwards in telling them. He was also decorated for bravery but never dwelled on it. I'm sure he looked on it as much as a family thing as a duty to his country.

I also had a medal and an honorable discharge, but only for getting wounded, not for being a hero. Morgan was a true American war hero. I also felt he was a hero because of the way he assimilated back into American society.

I had that in my mind when Morgan looked me straight in the eyes and said to me, "Kanook, I want you to know that I found something out in this past year and I want to share it with you." It was the same look he had in his eyes when he threatened to kill me a few years before. This evening's look also contained something else; it was a look of compassion that I had never noticed before. "Kanook," he said, "I want you to know that Jesus is alive today."

I almost fell off the porch swing when he said that. "You're joking, right?" I returned.

"No, I have never been more serious in my life," he said. We sat there and looked at each other and his expression never changed. I didn't know what to think. I had told him that I had become an assassin for a foreign government and he was coming up with this. After the shock wore off he began to delve into my past. He seemed fascinated when I told him about growing up in Canada and having to learn all the operas. He must have thought I was stringing him along a little bit. Marines are known for telling tall stories about sexual exploits and fast cars but this was a new one for him. He insisted that I sing something and the first thing that came to mind was "*Vesti la Giubba*" from "Pagliacci." I certainly was not an opera singer but I could belt out a few lines to get the message across.

He was dumfounded. It was a part of me that he had never known about and frankly wouldn't have believed. He joked and said, "If I knew you sounded that bad I would have shot you back in 'The Nam' and put you out of your misery."

He then probed me even further and when the subject of "Faust" came up and I told him that "I must have sold my soul to the Devil a hundred times," he stopped me. A sudden change came over his demeanor and he made me go over what I had just said. It meant nothing to me but it meant everything to him. He got up off the porch swing and walked into the house and came out with a Bible in his hand.

"Oh shit, what did I say?" came out of my mouth. Morgan had a look of horror on his face now.

"Don't you see what happened back then?" he said.

"It was just a play, it didn't mean nothin'," I said. He told me I was wrong, that it meant everything. I had opened up the door to the Devil and that was why I had no meaning or purpose in my life. He went on to tell me that the Devil had clouded my vision as a child and led me down a path of destruction. He said I needed to confess my sins and be baptized to be saved. I looked hard at him and thought, what has happened to this guy, he's gone crazy. I told him that I needed to find a gun show not a church. This set him to preaching about how Jesus had won us this victory and the "eye for an eye and tooth for a tooth" was not right anymore. We had to learn to turn the other cheek. It was quite a night. By the time we were all talked out I was ready to crawl into the bed his mother had made up for me and fall asleep.

The next day Morgan was off to college and I just hung around the house with his mom. She was nothing like my own mother. My mom back in Canada was a professional and Morgan's mom was a stay at home, keep the home fires burning kind of mom. I sat at the kitchen table and she talked all morning. She was so proud of her son and her husband and her country. She went on about everything that had happened in the county in the year since I had been gone.

She was doubly proud that "Morgan has come to the Lord and has himself a charge." I had never heard of a charge. It was his position as a lay minister up in Calhoun County at Mt. Liberty Baptist Church.

When Morgan returned from school we went on a long walk up the holler along Jessie's Run, the name of the creek that ran down the middle of the valley. We continued where we had left off the night before. We both started to cry when the names of our fallen comrades came up and he insisted that I pray with him. He was also very interested in Israel and the Jewish people and confessed to me he didn't know even one Jew in the whole county. It was, however, his conviction that Israel would factor very prominently in the near future in relation to biblical prophesy.

He was insistent that I renounce my mission and come to Jesus and get baptized. He said there was an outdoor baptism in a pond slated for the upcoming weekend and he would be assisting the pastor.

I explained to him that there was no turning back from what I was doing. I went on to explain that if I crossed these people that they would track me down wherever I was and kill me. I told him about Ben and how he would do it without even being asked. I said that this was Mossad we were talking about and how they followed me all over Manhattan for a month and I never had a clue. Their capabilities were beyond anything we had been trained for in the corps and the only reason they even bothered with me was because of my Canadian citizenship and the fact that I wasn't averse to killing.

We walked back down the holler to the house in time to greet his girlfriend as she drove up. I could see why Morgan was in love. She had that southern belle appearance and was just glowing. I was really feeling like an outsider now; these people had something that I just didn't possess. She stayed for dinner and left not long after we ate. I was sure that Morgan had told her that he needed more time with me, and being strong a Christian girl she obviously knew the drill.

That evening Morgan made me tell him over and over what Avi had told me about the Syrian tank corps and how they had stopped just north of Hushniyeh. It was a fact that I couldn't explain. I personally thought Avi had been suffering from shellshock and what he saw was only in his mind but for Morgan this was a biblical prophesy and I was somehow involved. The comet story also fascinated him except the part where we had killed the three soldiers with our knives and another eight with hand grenades and small arms fire. He also thought it was providential that we had been saved by the IDF from being killed. I could see he read much more into the event than I did. I thought if he had gone through the debriefing that I had he might have seen it differently. I was convinced that everything was weird but not all explainable and what the Israeli officers had told me about the atmospheric conditions made the most sense of all. Morgan wasn't convinced at all by my down playing both incidents.

When it was time to go to sleep I could tell this wasn't the place for me any more. In the past we would have killed or died for each other but times had changed and he had learned to move on. Morgan would have done anything for me but my destiny was not like his. It was only too obvious that he wasn't happy about what I had got myself into but we had a Marine Corps bond that was even stronger than his newfound faith and he would help out an old buddy no matter what.

"I don't like what you are doing," he said the next morning, "and I'll only help you because of Semper Fi." He then got on the phone to a cousin who was a member of the NRA. He said that he knew where every gun show in the country was located along with the times and the dates. When he got off the phone he told me his cousin lived down by the Ohio River in Parkersburg, "P-Burg," he called it, and there was a gun and knife show being held at the National Guard Armory starting the following Monday and running for a whole week. "Now you will have to stay and hear me preach," he said with a cunning smile. It wasn't until later that evening that it dawned on me that this was his way of finding more time to work on me.

I went to the college the next day with him hoping to see some of the veterans that I had met the year before when I was attending classes. I thought I would feel a little out of place but there were so many veterans hanging around outside of the classes I felt right at home. Some of the guys had their bush hats on and lots of them were wearing partial uniforms. They were a ragtag bunch. It reminded me of the Israeli reserves who were always showing up at the kibbutz wearing partial uniforms. It was, however, not an indication of the fighting capabilities of either group of people. I recognized a lot of the guys and had to come up with a story for them. They knew I had left school abruptly and where I was going and all of them wanted to hear my story. There were veterans from all the services, not all of them having served in Vietnam. Some had been posted in Germany and a couple from the U.S. Air Force had been posted in Thailand but we were brothers all the same.

The one question I had to invariably answer was, am I coming back to school? My new lying nature kicked in when that question was asked and I told them that I had found a good job up in Canada. I was even asked by a fellow marine vet, "Did ya git ya some over there?"

I gave him a wink and a nod before I back-tracked and jokingly said, "No."

I knew this guy had been with the 26th at Khe Sahn and had undergone months of bombardment and I didn't want to get him started. I looked into his eyes and kind of shuddered, wondering if I looked like that.

I had to wait two more days for Sunday morning to roll around before climbing into my fancy suit and shoes and along with the whole family we drove over to Calhoun County for the service at Mt. Liberty Baptist. The church was located up a long winding road and sat right at the top of the mountain. It was only open in the summer months and this was going to be the last service of the year. There was a church social planned and picnic tables were scattered around the area. The little church was filled to capacity and Morgan led the singing. I had never experienced anything like it in my life. Then it was time for him to give the sermon and I was brought to tears, not because of my emotions, but because I felt nothing when I heard Morgan's beautiful words. People in the crowd were crying out loud saying things like, "I'm going to see my daddy over yonder." I was relieved when it was over and we all filed outside for the picnic.

Morgan made a point of introducing me to all of the single girls at the gathering and each and every one I would compare to Ariela. It didn't matter and wasn't really fair. I had been fighting the idea but it struck me then that even though she treated me like a non-person I was in love with her.

I had my mind made up after the service that if there was ever a religion for me it would be Judaism. I was hooked on the idea of revenge, and the thought of forgiveness was just not for me. I remembered all of the Catholic masses I had to attend as a child and looking up at Jesus hanging on the cross and wondering if he was God why he would let a bunch of hicks do that to him. I was also still pissed at the nuns for turning me into the cops when I thought I was defending their honor. And even though there was no one in the world I would ever respect more than Morgan, I was still trying to digest the statement about Jesus being alive today. Also with the current of emotion running through the service and me feeling nothing, I thought back to Tel Aviv and that officer telling me I had a personality defect. I wondered if this was proof of his observations because I couldn't get swept up in the current of emotion.

I knew one thing and that was the fact that I was different from these people and more like the team of killers that had my loyalty. If these people knew I was a member of a squad of assassins planning a revenge killing with little or no emotion, they would all be horrified. For that matter, Morgan was a little horrified but he knew the rush of killing, he was one of America's best. I could see that he was going out of his way to show me that it could all be left behind if I wanted to move on. I just didn't know how to move on. Like the moth to a flame I was moving closer to the fire.

On Monday morning Morgan decided to take a day off from school and drive with me down to Parkersburg. It was the beginning of fall and some of the leaves on the trees were starting to change color. West Virginia was glorious in the autumn season and the drive through the valleys was a pleasure. When we arrived at "P-Burg" we drove straight to his cousin's house.

His cousin Baxter was a big man, bigger than me and he worked at a chemical plant on the Ohio side of the river. He was not a veteran but a member of the NRA and a real gun nut. He didn't flinch when Morgan told him what I was looking for. Coming down from Canada he knew about our gun laws and thought I was just going into the illegal gun trade. This didn't bother him a bit. "As long as you don't break any of our laws I'll help you all I can," he said. "I have a table at the show myself but I don't have any of the hardware you're looking for." He had us help him carry some shotguns and rifles out to his pickup truck. We then climbed into my car and followed him across town to the show.

When we arrived at the armory the parking lot was full. There were cars from all over the South; license tags from as far away as Texas and Missouri. People were filing in with guns slung over their shoulders and side arms in holsters. It was quite a sight.

We helped Baxter set up at his table before we went looking around. The building had every kind of gun imaginable and we settled in at the handgun section. I could see at a glance that I would be able to fill out my list and started with the

.22 revolvers. They were mostly the long-barreled Colt models and I knew I had to stay away from them. I found two with short barrels at the first table I attended and was encouraged by the owner to try them out.

They had a section of the armory out in the back roped off with sandbags and targets where the small caliber weapons could be tested. Morgan and I, along with the owner of the guns, went out and fired off a few rounds. We also tested speed loaders and were satisfied.

I purchased two Colts at the first table and took them out and placed them in the trunk of the car. I didn't want to purchase all the weapons at the first table so I continued on. The next table I stopped at had some .9mm automatics, not the type preferred by the team but I went outside and gave them a try anyway.

The noise was awesome. There were gun enthusiasts all lined up like at the rifle range back at Camp Pendleton and all blasting away. I was happy with the feel of the action and along with several boxes of ammo I made my second purchase. I thought it would look fishy if I was to purchase all the guns on the list at the show but the place was so full of people I could have bought twice as many as I needed and no one would have cared.

By the end of the day my wrist was so sore it was aching but I didn't care. I had my list complete and we thanked Baxter and began our drive out of Parkersburg back to Gilmer County.

. Morgan, ever the patriot, told me there was just something I had to see before we hit the road and he made me drive down to the Ohio River where we parked the car. Morgan and I walked along the banks of the river until we came to a huge cement wall; it must have been several football fields long. I had never seen anything like it in my life. Up high on the wall was a plaque that read "Dedicated to Stonewall Jackson." Morgan beamed with pride when we stood before the wall and with a tear running down his cheek he snapped a salute, about faced, and marched on.

We had humped the boonies together but for me it was for my buddies. I now began to see where the difference lay. Morgan's traditions ran deep; God and country meant everything to him, whereas I was what Ben had told me with a burning gun pressed against my throat, nothing but a mercenary.

We marched together back along the river to where the car was parked, climbed in, and drove back up the mountains to Gilmer County. Morgan worked on me all the way trying to talk me into staying but I told him I knew too much and I could never hide from these people. Also there was Ariela and I couldn't get her off my mind.

The next day it was time to leave. Morgan's mom was crying, his dad was by her side, and he gave me a big hug and told me he would be praying for me. And with the trunk full of handguns and ammunition I turned the car around and headed down the holler and pointed it toward New York City. I didn't need to rush. I still had almost a week to meet up with Ariela at the park and I didn't want to get stopped by the police so I took my time, carefully watching my speed limit while driving along the interstate.

I knew the route by now and drove out of West Virginia through Pennsylvania, stopping at the same motel outside of Pittsburgh. That night while lying in bed I couldn't get the statement out of my mind that Morgan had said to me about Jesus being alive today. It made a little sense to me that perhaps the Devil was alive today but I just couldn't see where Jesus was.

CHAPTER ELEVEN

I arrived in New York late the next evening and parked the car at the same overnight parking garage. Then along with my fancy suit I hopped a New York taxi cab and rode over the bridge into Manhattan. I rented a room at the same hotel and fell into a deep sleep.

The next morning when I walked out of the hotel and into the mass of people on the street I don't know why but I felt safe. The weather was changing and the cool air made the walk to the park invigorating. There were already lots of chess matches underway and I engaged in one with one of the chess hustlers who I knew by name. I put up as good a fight as I could but was not even close to being a match for this guy. It didn't matter at all, the game took my mind off everything and I became lost in the moment.

When I had had enough chess I walked back to the hotel, stopping at my favorite street vendor for something to eat. All the time I wondered if I was being shadowed but gave up even trying to spot anyone. It was just impossible with the scores of people everywhere. That night I dressed up in my finest and walked out of the hotel heading to my favorite restaurant. I had barely hit the street when a car pulled up and the back door opened. I looked inside and sitting there was the most beautiful woman in the world. It was Ariela and she looked like a Hollywood movie star. She motioned me to get in, which I did without hesitation. I recognized the driver as David, one of the team members I hadn't seen since Tel Aviv. Ariela was unusually nice to me and asked if I was going out to eat and if I was would I like some company. I almost fainted.

David drove us to a restaurant I was unfamiliar with and dropped us off in the front of the building. Once inside the maitre d' showed us to a table and we sat down like a couple. I was floating on cloud nine. She, on the other hand, scolded me not to stare and make a fool of myself. Deep down I knew she was only following orders by being with me, but I was content to lie to myself, hoping that something would come of this night.

I asked her how she knew I was going to be outside the hotel when she drove by and she told me that she knew every move I was going to make even before I did. She told me the route I had traveled to West Virginia. She made one mistake, calling a "holler" a "hollow" when she described Morgan's parents' farm, but she was bang on with everything else. She knew Morgan's phone number and repeated almost word for word his entire conversation with Baxter. She went on to tell me the number of handguns I had purchased at the Parkersburg Gun and Knife Show, then in a moment of pure braggadocio she reached into her purse and pulled out a picture of Morgan and me standing in front of the wall along the banks of the Ohio River.

I asked her what the hell she needed me for if they had that kind of surveillance capability and she just grinned and replied that they had a really good infrastructure in the U.S. but until now there had never been a need to apply it to Canada and that's where I came in. She said they also had to know if the money in my bank account would change my attitude toward the mission.

"Did I pass the test?" I asked her and she just grinned.

I ordered a bottle of wine and feasted on a meal fit for a king, all the time trying not to drool over her. As much as she was all business I just couldn't help the way I felt. During the meal she handed me a piece of paper with a street address and instructed me to memorize the address and then destroy the paper. I was then ordered to deliver the car to the address, which was just a street corner. David would meet me there and take delivery of the car and the contents in the trunk. I was then to meet him at the same street corner the next day and pick up the car from him and then drive back to the farm in Blainville.

After the meal and another bottle of wine we walked out of the restaurant. I was feeling a little tipsy and while waiting for a taxi I got up my courage and proposed that she come back to my hotel with me. She batted her eyelashes and said in her best New York drawl, "Do you want I should spell it out fo' ya?" She then climbed into the first taxi cab that pulled up and told me she would see me back in Canada.

I was left standing alone in front of the restaurant half drunk and in a state of anger. "Get a good picture of this, you assholes," I said out loud and held my middle finger up for anyone to see. I didn't know which way it was back to the hotel and didn't care. I just started walking down the street. Feeling the effects of the wine I called out again, "Why don't you assholes at least give me a ride back to my hotel?" and walked on.

After an hour or so of walking around Manhattan I was completely lost and hailed a taxi cab and instructed the driver to take me back to my hotel. I decided that evening after delivering the car I would walk to my bank and make out a money order for Morgan for his wedding. He hadn't actually said he was going to get married but from every indication I got there would soon be a wedding and I wasn't sure if I would be around for it.

The next day I picked up the car and drove to the address on the paper. David was standing on the street corner. The night before he had been dressed in an impeccable suit but this morning he looked like a construction worker waiting for a ride to a work site. I pulled up at the street corner and he jumped in the passenger side. He told me to drive around the corner and then ordered me to get out. "I'll see you here at the same time tomorrow," he said and drove off. I still wasn't over the disappointment of the night before and tried to walk it off on my way to the bank.

When I finally reached the bank I had a money order for $1,000 made out to Morgan and then went looking for a place to buy an envelope and a stamp. When I had the letter posted I walked to Washington Square Park and found my favorite chess hustler and promptly lost some money to him. The game helped to relieve my heartache but deep down I was a wreck. I walked back to my hotel, stopping again for a hotdog at my favorite street vendor, and spent the rest of the day and evening watching television.

I was standing on the same spot David was the previous day when he pulled up in the car. He didn't bother driving around the corner; he just hopped out with the car still running and I climbed in the driver's seat. "I'll see you at the farm," he said and walked away.

I drove back to the car park, left the car, and took a cab back to my hotel and checked out. I gathered up my fancy clothes, took a taxi back across the bridge, picked up the car, and spent the next few hours trying to find the interstate that would take me north to Canada.

When I finally drove onto the interstate I pulled over at the first rest stop and looked in the trunk. I wasn't at ease thinking that all of those handguns were just sitting out in the open for any customs officer to see. I was relieved after I opened the trunk to see that it was empty. The rest of the drive was uneventful. When I finally pulled up to the United States—Canada border crossing and was questioned by the customs officer I was waved through without any problem.

I arrived at the farm quite late that evening and Ben, along with two other members of the team, was waiting for me. At first glance I recognized the other two agents but it struck me how they could all look so similar. They were not too short and not too tall, medium in everything except that they had that unmistakable Middle Eastern look.

Ben ordered one of the agents to go out to the car. He immediately picked up a box of tools and a flashlight and walked out of the door. The other agent followed while I was debriefed by Ben. I was a little sarcastic with him pointing out how Ariela had run down everything I had done in the past two weeks. We went through the procedure anyway. That was my homecoming celebration.

In about a half an hour the agents returned to the house with fourteen handguns and four hundred rounds of ammunition. "Where did those come from?" I asked, to which there was no reply. They laid the guns out on the kitchen table and one by one gave them all a thorough inspection.

The three of them picked out the guns that they preferred, with each picking a .22 revolver and a 9mm automatic. It reminded me of when I was a kid and when my coach passed around our soccer uniforms. The agents must have felt half naked up till this moment and I thought I would pick a couple out for myself when Ben stopped me and told me that I wouldn't be needing one. I might be a member of this team but certainly not an equal one.

Ben then ordered us all to get some sleep and told me we would be driving into Montreal the next day to purchase another car and start looking for another apartment. I crawled into my sleeping bag and had no problem falling asleep on the couch where I had slept before. Ben went out to sleep in the truck while one of the agents got the bed and the other was on the floor next to my couch.

The next morning we ate breakfast together and I could sense that things were beginning to become serious. It reminded me of a briefing I had attended when I was with marine recon. We were a group of killers who were onto our prey and nothing was going to stop us. Ben asked one of the agents if he had put the car back together properly and he said he had and with that we finished our meal and Ben and I walked out of the door and climbed into the car for the drive into Montreal. While driving into the city Ben said that after I bought another car he wanted me to phone the theatrical company and make sure I was on the list to audition for the play. The idea of the play had truly slipped my mind, probably because I wasn't all that crazy about the idea, but I agreed anyway.

When we got within a block of the car lot, Ben handed me an envelope and told me to find another car like the other two but to make sure it was a different color. Then he told me to meet him back at the apartment. When I walked onto the car lot the old salesman grinned and said, "Hey, you're back, I haven't heard of any bank robberies so you must be doing something right." He asked if I was looking for another car and how much I wanted to spend. We went through the same thing for a fourth time and I drove off the car lot. "Take care of yourself, kid," he said, smiling as I drove away.

When I put the key in the lock at the apartment in West Montreal and walked in, the sights and smells told me that the place had been lived in. There were maps pinned up on the walls with pencil marks and arrows. There were also lots of pictures on the walls just like the one Ariela had shown me in the restaurant in New York of me and Morgan. The pictures were all of people, some sitting at outdoor cafés, some in crowds. There were circles drawn around some of the faces which had obviously undergone intensive scrutiny. There were cardboard boxes opened up and electronic equipment exposed.

Ben was sitting at the kitchen table with other members of the team. They were all inspecting the handguns I had bought in the United States. In the first display of humor I had seen since this had all started they all raised their weapons and pretended to shoot me. I'm sure it was scripted because it brought a little levity to the room.

When I saw one of them was a woman my heart raced, thinking it was Ariela, but it was the other female member of the team, Leah. "Here's Iago now," said one of the men sitting at the table. I remembered his name from Tel Aviv; he called himself Yigal. Ben, now all business, asked about the car and where it was parked and instructed me to hand over the keys. He then told me to go out and buy a newspaper and start looking for another apartment.

As I left the building I started to feel a pain in my stomach. I bought the newspaper and returned to the apartment telling Ben I wasn't feeling well. In their characteristic efficiency he instructed Leah to take a look at me. "She's a doctor," he said, as though it was nothing.

The pain started getting worse and I had to lie down on a couch. The men at the table didn't pay me any mind and Leah began giving me a physical examination.

She announced to Ben that she thought I was having a gall bladder attack and I would need some attention. Ben was unsympathetic and told her to get me into the bedroom and do what she had to. I made my way into the bedroom and lay on the bed in pain. Ben came in after a while and asked what we should do. She said I would either require surgery or there was an old witch's brew she could try that required a few things from the store. I was in such pain I hardly remember the rest of the day. She made me drink a horrible concoction that made me violently ill with vomiting and diarrhea and I finally fell asleep.

The next morning I was feeling weak but the intense pain I had experienced in my stomach was gone. Leah brought me some herbal tea and my copy of Shakespeare plays and said it was time for me to start to study. "Ben wants you to be out there and visible," she said with a little bit of sympathy, "so you must know that play by heart." I lay in bed the rest of the day looking through the book without the energy to really apply myself.

From the bedroom I could hear the team planning a grid pattern of the city. I was surprised to find out that they really hadn't a clue where the targets might be at that moment. I could tell that they had picked out an apartment building and they were going to put it under twenty-four-hour surveillance. They had the pickup and camper loaded with electronic gear and parked at a location where the building could be observed.

When I felt a little better I went into the living room in time to see one of the team members coming out of the other bedroom with some pictures like the ones on the walls. They were still wet, from which I gathered they had set up a darkroom in the other bedroom. They called this agent Yonnie and he began pinning up the pictures. Every picture that he attached to the wall was studied intensely by the other team members. They took turns looking at the pictures with a large magnifying glass and comparing them to a picture that was lying on the table.

I was not invited to join in on this and was content to sit and watch. They were totally concentrated on the pictures on the wall when Ben looked over at me and asked if I was up to looking for another apartment that day. I begged off. I just hung around the rest of the day trying to stay out of the way while team members came and went. In the meantime Leah made a chicken soup she called "Jewish penicillin" and served me a bowl. Ben, in his sarcastic way, told me if that didn't fix me up they might have to cancel my contract.

I finally felt up to looking through the paper and there in the entertainment section again was the notice for auditions for "Othello." "Hey, there it is again," I said with no one listening. I then got Ben's attention and asked where he wanted me to look for another apartment. He then looked away from the pictures pinned on the wall and walked over to the map of Montreal Island. He stood looking at the map for a few minutes, picked out a spot, and placed his finger on the map. "Right here," he said. I got up to get a better look and to study the names of the streets intersecting where his finger was pointing. It was at the opposite end of the island where we now found ourselves and in the French-speaking part of the city.

I told him it would be a little harder for me because it was all French over there and he said, "Take Ariela with you. She can translate and pretend to be your wife."

I sat back on the couch with a piercing jolt running through my body. I couldn't even hear her name without reacting.

"That should give you a thrill," he said, obviously making fun of me and my crush on her. I heard some of the team snicker at his remark, which didn't make me feel any better. I felt a twinge of embarrassment and asked when she would be back from New York to which he replied, "She's up at the farm. You can go and pick her up tomorrow or when you are feeling up to it." He then told me to buy a French paper to take up to the farm with me so she could go over it.

Leah brought me another bowl of her "Jewish penicillin" and I was on the road to recovery. She said she had not seen many people my age having a gall bladder attack but that is what she suspected was my trouble. I was impressed at how professional she could be and so nurturing at the same time. I was thinking to myself, could she nurse me back to health and then slit my throat if ordered to?

I knew I had to get a grip on my feelings for Ariela. If I had a puppy love type crush on her that wasn't reciprocated in the slightest it could somehow lead to trouble. I knew I was becoming the brunt of the rest of the team's jokes so I decided I was going to make a point of keeping my feelings in check from that moment on.

I was up early the next day and Yonnie handed me back the set of keys for my latest acquisition. He was the only member of the team in the apartment; the rest were out setting up surveillance. He told me Ben wanted me to return when I had viewed the apartments with my report. I then left the apartment and headed over the bridge, out of the city north toward Blainville.

When I reached the farm the cool autumn weather was starting to feel like winter. Inside the farmhouse the wood stove was burning and the atmosphere here couldn't have been more different from that of the city. In the apartment in the city everything was set up for surveillance whereas here the mood was homey. Ariela was in the kitchen looking as different as could be from a few days before in New York. She grinned in a coquettish manner and my big ruse was blown away. "Made it back from New York alright?" she asked. I replied that I had and then she said, "So we are supposed to be husband and wife now?"

I thought she must be as cruel as Ben. "Ya, just pretending, I guess. We better get going," I said. I knew my cover was blown and she and the team now had a way to control me without the slightest bit of trouble. I hated myself at that moment, hated my weakness, knowing I was vulnerable to these emotions. "I have a newspaper you can go over on our way into the city," I said and I turned and walked out to the car.

On the drive into Montreal Ariela picked out three possible ads and we stopped at a coffee shop where we ordered some breakfast and she used the telephone. She came back to the table and told me that we had three appointments to view apartments that day. We spent the rest of the time over breakfast thinking up a good story as to what we were going to tell the landlord.

We left the restaurant and drove to the first apartment that was on her list. After driving around the area Ariela said that she wasn't even going to bother to go in and view the place. "I don't like the access in the front or the back," she said, along with several other points that she was firm about. "Let's go and look at the next one," she said and read me off the address.

"Hey, this is kind of like being married, isn't it?" I joked, and she reminded me not to get any funny ideas.

The second suite on the list was perfect. We cruised around the area before we even bothered to knock on the landlord's door. Ariela liked the area; the traffic flow and access was what she was looking for. When we finally pushed the buzzer I saw a different person in Ariela that I hadn't noticed before. Along with speaking French like a Québécois she had a charm that any landlord couldn't refuse. I could only understand a few of the words from the conversation, my high school French had left me so limited. The landlord hardly even noticed me anyway.

This girl has it all, I thought. I don't know if I can take this.

One of the criteria that Ben insisted on was that the building had to have enough apartments so that a nosy landlord wouldn't have the time to notice the traffic that would be coming and going from the premises. This building was barely big enough. When we finally viewed the suite and signed the lease I don't think the landlord even noticed I didn't speak the language. We left the building with the keys and the landlord in a daze.

When we climbed into the car I asked Ariela what they were talking about and she said she had told him she was a graduate student at McGill University. She also said that she explained to the landlord that she would be tutoring some undergraduates at the apartment so there would be some foreign students coming and going. I could tell that the landlord had taken it all in and who wouldn't, I thought. It certainly sounded believable to me. Then I asked what she had told him about me and she replied, "I told him that you were just one of my students who was kind enough to drive me around."

"One of your students?" I said, feeling hurt. "I thought I was supposed to be your husband?"

She then went on saying that she didn't think that the husband—wife story was going to work, "and besides, I just don't think you could handle it emotionally."

"What the fuck are you talking about?" I replied.

She then was as firm as I had ever seen her. "We are on a mission for our history and our people and you are just a paid mercenary. We are not children and we will not allow your childish emotions to jeopardize the outcome. Now drive to the other apartment. Ben is waiting for us."

I was definitely put in my place and to keep the conversation going I asked her how she came up with the story as it wasn't anything that we had talked about over breakfast and she said it just came to her as we drove past the university.

When we walked into the first apartment I could see why we needed another place. It was getting rather crowded. The agents present were feverishly going over pictures and maps and fiddling with electronic gear. Most of them never even looked up when we came in.

Ariela gave her report to Ben and without hesitation he ordered her and one of the male agents to move across the island to the new apartment. I handed my car keys to Ariela and she along with Yonnie began to gather things up for the move. "You can help them pack the boxes out to the car," Ben told me and returned to his work.

After Ariela and Yonnie left Leah came up to me and asked how I was feeling. She gave me a quick examination and pronounced me well.

When the team members finished studying the new pictures they all filled their pockets with rolls of film and left the apartment. Ben then had time to focus his attention on me. "It's only a week until it's time to audition for that play. I want you to be ready," he said, and then he handed me a photo of a man and a woman. "I want you to study this picture and then you and I are going shopping." I looked over the picture for a few minutes and then Ben said, "Let's go."

We drove to a commercial area of Montreal where Ben dropped me off, telling me that there was a bakery at the end of the street. "Go in there and buy some bread and try to make some small talk with anyone who serves you. I want them to remember you. You got it?" Then he said, "Keep in mind those photos." This made me feel more than just an outsider. I was actually doing something that made me feel like a secret agent and not just kitchen help. "I'll meet you back here," he said and drove off into the traffic.

I walked the rest of the way to the end of the street, aware that all the window dressings were in either French or in Arabic script. "This should be good for a laugh," I said out loud to myself as I entered the bakery.

Immediately upon entering the shop the smells of baked goods overwhelmed me. It wasn't a very big space but it was cluttered with display cabinets filled with pastries and sweets that I had never seen before. There were flat breads as well as buns and loaves stacked on top of the cabinets. All over the walls were posters of what looked to me to be Middle Eastern movie stars and pop stars and the place was loud with the unmistakable sound of music that must have been performed by one of the people pictured on the wall. I waited in line thinking I should be taking French lessons and not wasting my time getting ready for a bloody Shakespeare play that I probably wouldn't even get a part in.

When I reached the head of the line and it was my turn to order I was served by a young lady who greeted me with a friendly "bonjour." She had all the appearances of Middle Eastern descent and looked to me to be not that dissimilar from Ariela and Leah. I had to order in English, which she switched to with ease. It made me feel ignorant and angry and took me back to my failure to apply myself in French class at school.

I purchased some buns from her but was sure I had failed to make the impression that Ben had requested. Other than just another "Anglo" I could not have made any impression. When I returned to the corner where Ben had dropped me from the car I was picked up with his usual perfect timing.

Once back in the car Ben went over and over with me what I had observed in the shop. He wanted to know every detail, which I couldn't provide. He was insistent that I would have to do much better the next time I entered this store and any other place he sent me into.

After that we returned to the apartment. I had not been back at the apartment more than a few minutes when Yonnie and Leah returned and immediately Yonnie went into the bedroom. Ben began to debrief me again, this time along with Leah, going over and over what I had told him in the car.

Then Yonnie came out of the bedroom with a handful of wet photographs that he began to pin up on the wall. There were pictures of me stepping out of the car and walking down the avenue. Photos of people on the street and finally pictures of me entering and exiting the bakery. Ben brought out his magnifying glass and went over each photo slowly and methodically. While he was doing this Leah sat me down and placed another picture in front of me and instructed me to study it. "Did you see anyone who looked like this?" I was asked. I felt as though I had let them down, not having a positive answer for them. But if I had learned one thing with these people there was no point in trying to bullshit them because they could almost read my thoughts.

When they had studied the pictures and were satisfied that today wasn't the day, Ben informed me that the other team was set up in a different location and we were going to go through the same thing again. We left Yonnie and Leah in the apartment and drove to the same part of Montreal just down the street from the bakery. This time it was a restaurant and I was instructed to go in and order a nice meal and take as much time as I needed.

Before Ben dropped me off a good distance from the restaurant he went over more details on how to observe and remember. I already had been trained as a child to remember but those were just songs and words; this was very new to me. Deep down I hated Ben but on this day I started to see he was a teacher as well as a soldier and my fear of him started to turn to respect. He told me what to look for and to make myself a mental note of things. He also told me how many times to get up and go to the washroom. He pointed out ways to start small talk with the waiters and how to get around the language barrier. I realized then that I was in school and being trained by one of the best. As I got out of the car and walked the rest of the way to the restaurant I was reminded that if I didn't look like a western farm boy I would be of no use to these people and would probably be working in a mine or sawmill.

When I entered the restaurant I immediately wished I had dressed up in my spiffy duds. I seemed to have only two appearances: one my fancy suit and the other the way I looked at the time, somewhat like a yokel. I could see that I was completely out of place and would never be able to fit in. The atmosphere inside was Middle Eastern with the smells and the music. I was greeted warmly by a waiter who seemed a little too friendly for my liking, who seated me close to the bar. The waiter was as fruity as one could get, short and pudgy and balding and swaying his ass like a girl. I wondered if he was putting on an act for me or if that was his normal posture. I played along with his game, all the time taking note of everything I could.

I ordered what the waiter recommended along with a bottle of wine. I was never a good drinker and the wine loosened me up a little too much. I think I gave the waiter the wrong impression or it was the only thing he had on his mind but when it was time to leave he was ready to give me a kiss. This revolted me and I paid the check and left.

I was half drunk when I left the place, and when I got back into the car with Ben I was fuming. "Give me a gun, I want to go back and shoot that prick," I said as soon as Ben began to debrief me in the car. Ben screamed at me and we began to scuffle in the car. I was drunk and never could hold my liquor and for the second time Ben reached into his belt and drew his side arm. Like the time before he held the gun at

my throat and repeated what he said on the driving course in
Tel Aviv. I was frustrated and clearly out of my depth doing
this kind of work. I had overstepped the line and had to be
trained better for this part of the mission.

When I finally calmed down we drove back to the
apartment and I sat around and pouted like a child. Ben
and Leah went into the other room obviously discussing
my behavior and what to do about it. It was the only time
I had heard them speaking in Hebrew since they arrived in
Montreal; Hebrew was totally forbidden so I knew this was
serious. I could hear them throwing in Ariela's name in the
midst of the conversation and that didn't help me a bit.

When they emerged from their emergency meeting Leah
came over to me and reassured me that we would get past
this. She told me that she was aware of the hostility between
me and Ben and they had decided that because there was so
much work ahead of us and this was the most critical part
of the operation that I would be working with Ariela from
now on. It was as if they were pacifying a little child. She also
insisted that I apologize to Ben for my lack of self-control,
and from that moment forward I was expressly forbidden to
drink any alcohol for the remainder of the mission.

I had no problem saying I was sorry to Ben. What was I
to think, one minute I was looking to him as my mentor and
teacher and the next I was acting like a drunken fool. We
agreed to put it all behind us and went back to work. Ben then
began to debrief me all over again telling me that I would
have to go back into the restaurant again and jokingly said
that when the mission was over I could kill the waiter if I so
chose. Once I was sober I didn't have the same homophobic
attitude and thought that killing the little fag was somewhat
drastic.

The next day Ariela showed up at the apartment and after
a meeting with the other team members we were on our way
to the same Arabic area of Montreal. Today it was a grocery
store and I was feeling somewhat embarrassed about the day

before and Ariela picked on me all the way across town. "We are not children," she said. "You could put this whole mission in jeopardy with behavior like that." It really didn't bother me to have her scolding me, I was just happy to be sitting beside her in the car. I would do anything that was required of me now. I was too young to realize I was really emotionally immature. I was a veteran and a killer but just like a little child sitting beside her.

As Ben had done the day before she dropped me off a block away from the place I was to reconnoiter and I was in and out of the store and back in the car in only a few minutes. She again had to scold me like a child telling me that I couldn't have done a good enough job in only a few minutes in the store and I had better get my act together.

Back in the apartment Ben did the debriefing and he echoed Ariela's complaint about my not spending enough time in the store. When will I ever do anything right with these people? I thought, but was determined to do better.

The next day when the team met discussing the day's activities Ben reminded me that the auditions for the play were coming up in a couple of days and I had better be ready. This was the one thing I had no worries about. I said that I had had enough acting lessons in the last couple of days to make it a lock that I would get a part. Ben then said, "Not just any part will do, I want you to play Iago. I want everyone to know who you are and what you are doing here and don't worry about getting the part. We can arrange a little accident for anyone who gets in your way."

CHAPTER TWELVE

I wasn't one for getting overly nervous but when I walked into the Montreal Repertory Theatre the next night I was in a state of paranoia. I was expecting a small high school type gymnasium and a bunch of no talent hacks trying to step outside of their class but I couldn't have been farther from the truth. When I walked up the aisle of the grand theatre and looked at the crowd gathered on the stage I wanted to turn around and run away. There were about thirty people, men and women of all ages milling about on the stage talking and laughing, and in the centre of the crowd was a black man whose voice could be heard above all the rest. You could see he had a charisma about him and when the time came he quieted the crowd and looked everyone over like he was at a cattle auction. I joined in with the crowd but felt out of place. He welcomed the gathering as a whole and then one by one in a very personal manner. Many of the people he knew by name and he exchanged pleasantries with them, and the ones he didn't know he asked our names and where we were from.

He then had everyone sit in chairs in a large circle and

had a young lady pass out books with "Othello, The Moor of Venice" written across the front in bold letters.

The black man stood in the centre of the circle and announced that he was the director and was also going to be playing the part of Othello. He then went on to explain to the people who were there to audition that he didn't expect such a large turn out and everyone would get a fair chance to win a part. He then went over the story line for anyone who wasn't familiar with it and began to read the opening act. He had everyone read a line or two until the entire circle had read a few lines. When it came time for a woman's part to be read and it was a man's turn he insisted that the man read it anyway. "In Shakespeare's time all the actors were men," he bellowed and insisted we continue.

When it came to my turn I read my part but could tell that I was just a face in the crowd. It was obvious that some of the actors were going to be his favorites when he called them by name and allowed them to read longer than the rest of us.

I knew from my childhood that the play consisted of several minor parts and only a couple of major parts and he had already announced that he was going to play one of the lead parts himself. "I'll be lucky to win any part," I thought. I was sure he already had his cast made up in his mind.

Before the evening was over he had everyone stand and read from the book a few more lines but as things dragged on I came to believe it was going to be hopeless to get noticed.

When it came to be my turn, he picked a part in a latter section of the play and gave me a prompt and I recited the lines by heart. I didn't get them word for word but it turned everyone's head and caught his attention. I could see from the crowd that I hadn't impressed anyone and I had started an atmosphere of petty jealousy.

"You have read the play before?" the director remarked without any fanfare and moved on to the next person.

The evening ended after everyone had had their chance to make an impression on the director. Before we broke up he insisted we all return the next evening to continue the audition.

I walked back to the apartment not knowing what to say to Ben about my chances, more than a little depressed about the prospects. Ben and Leah were home and they debriefed me as though I had been out on a combat mission. This was standard procedure, I knew, but I had been so wrapped up in the audition that I had forgotten my real reason for being in Montreal in the first place.

Ben was writing notes as I ran down the entire evening. He made me try to remember every face and especially the ones who were the director's favorites. I told him that I didn't remember any names. I was too nervous and intimidated by the place. He assured me it wouldn't be a problem. He then ordered Leah to gather one of the teams together for the next evening. He wanted all the names, addresses, where the people worked, phone numbers, pictures, sexual preference, everything. Then he told her to have Yonnie bug the phone of the director. He wanted to know what the man was thinking.

Then, like turning off a light bulb, Ben changed the subject and told me about the two places that I was to visit the next day with Ariela. He then changed the subject again and began giving me a lecture on sexuality. "You know you are going to have to get over this problem you have with homosexuals," he said. He went on to tell me the world was full of them and in the theatre I would probably run into one or two. He said that we were getting close to fulfilling our mission and now was not the time to ruin it because of some stupid phobia. Ben was as soft as he could be but I knew he wasn't kidding.

I told him it would never be a problem in the future and then took my chance to throw in a jab. "You're not fag are you?" For the first time we had a real belly laugh. First Leah, then Ben, and then me, we laughed until there were tears coming down our cheeks.

Ariela was early the next day and Ben gave us our orders for that morning. He had some intelligence he wouldn't discuss in front of me about the restaurant and had me dropped off for breakfast there. I was just happy to be with Ariela in any capacity, even if my love affair with her was only one-sided. The queer waiter who had taken a fancy to me wasn't working that morning so it was easier for me to do my duty and take note of anyone I saw.

After breakfast I was driven back to the apartment and debriefed in the usual manner, only this time I was given additional pictures to view. When I announced to Ben that I might have recognized one of the photos he, along with Ariela and Leah, became as excited as I had ever seen them. They made me go over and over the photo and then they made me walk through my breakfast again and again. By the time we were finished I was exhausted, totally confused, and not sure of anything. I only had the one mission that day except for the rehearsal in the evening that I was dreading. I went to Ben and tried to beg off the whole initiative and he climbed all over me. "We are the secret here, not you," he said. "You must have a story that will pass any scrutiny whereas we are not even here." He went on to chastise me in front of the other members of the team until again I had to eat crow and apologize for trying to wimp out.

That evening when I walked into the playhouse the thought struck me, I wonder if my father ever sang here, and I thought how ironic it would be if he had. Then I looked around and I was taken back to my childhood and the times I had spent in the Queen Elizabeth Theatre in Vancouver. I got up my courage and said to myself, I can handle this, and walked up to the stage where all the actors were milling about and the director was holding court.

After a few minutes he politely asked everyone to sit down and instead of reading lines he began to run down the theme of the play. He started with the main characters and one by one he gave an overview of the personalities and proclivities of everyone. It was then I realized that I may have been familiar with the words of the story but I had a child's interpretation and was ignorant of the true tragedy. At the same time I looked around and thought what a shock it would be if these civilians knew they were under the intense scrutiny of the Israeli Intelligence Service and soon I would know their darkest secrets.

After a quick overview of the minor characters the director then went into the personalities of Othello and Iago; one being a scheming liar and the other an honorable victim. It was all a little intense for everyone until the director, who along with being a great actor, director, and a Shakespearian scholar, went into his interpretation as to why Iago was such a devilish character. He said he believed Iago had an unrequited homosexual love for Othello, which got everyone's attention.

"Oh shit," I grumbled, which sent a few glances my way. The director harrumphed and shot me a glance and continued. I immediately smiled and focused my attention on the director who went on with his talk.

After he finished he separated the group into the people who he obviously knew and favored for the main characters and the rest of us who would make up non-speaking parts. He then had us look on while he went through the first act with the players he had chosen. After a couple of hours of this we broke and refreshments were served. It was then I noticed a young lady taking pictures of the cast—her camera flashing and all the actors taking turns being photographed. When she came to me and lifted her camera I noticed behind all the gaudy makeup, glasses, and wig that it was Ariela and my heart sank. She gave me a wink, took my picture, and moved on. The director then dismissed the entire cast and requested we return the next evening.

I walked back to the apartment while Ariela obviously rode along with someone from the team who remained invisible. I was anxious to hear and see what the team had come up with even if they had barely had time to do their thing. I

wasn't disappointed when I arrived back at the apartment.
Yonnie was already pinning the still wet photographs up on
the wall and Ben had a transcript of the director's telephone
conversation with the actress who was to play Desdemona.
The conversation was from the previous night but was almost
entirely about the play and the actors. I was even mentioned;
he called me a no-talent pretentious bastard who would be
lucky to make it as a stagehand. When I heard that I asked
Ben if it would be OK for me to put a bomb in his car when
it was all over and he told me not to worry, that he had called
me worse.

   We then analyzed the man who the director had tapped to
play the villain Iago. The man was a high school principal who
had performed in other plays with this cast and was not only a
proven actor but a personal friend of the director. There was
no one even mentioned for his understudy. Ben told Ariela to
give this job to Yigal, one of her team members. "I don't want
you to kill him," he said, "just give him a little nudge with the
car." With that Ben changed the subject and we discussed the
next day's work.

   It was back to the bakery the next day and then lunch at
the restaurant. The queer waiter was working and he made
a point of serving me. On this occasion I stayed away from
the wine and finished my lunch, all the while looking and
listening although I couldn't understand any of the language
being spoken in the background. After lunch I stopped by the
grocery store and bought a few things, then was picked up by
Ariela and driven back to the apartment to be debriefed.

   It seemed to me that we were getting nowhere but while
I was doing my thing with Ariela the other team was taking
pictures and bugging telephones all over Montreal. There
seemed to no end to the photos and transcripts that Leah
and Ben were constantly going over. It seemed that every time
I entered and left the apartment Yonnie was coming out of
the darkroom with more wet pictures and then pinning them
up on the wall. The walls were beginning to look like a pin

cushion from the photos constantly going up and coming down.

When I walked into the theatre that evening the crowd wasn't as boisterous as on the previous occasions and when the director got everyone's attention he announced that one of the cast members had been in a terrible accident and was in the hospital. It seemed that he was involved in a hit and run accident and had multiple fractures of his legs and arms. The director sadly announced that he would need to recast the part of Iago.

How ironic, I thought. I wonder if the pretentious no-talent bastard will get a chance.

I certainly wasn't the director's first choice; he had all the remaining men including the ones who had been reading for the minor parts give it a go. You could see that the director wasn't impressed with any of us but I could see that I had a leg up on all the others simply because the part was daunting and I happened to know it by heart already. The rehearsal that evening ended early without the director announcing his decision. We were not required to meet again for a few days but in the meantime he requested all the males to study the part.

When I got back to the apartment that evening it was business as usual. Ben and Leah were going over transcripts and photos and Ariela was there making a late meal for the team. When I walked in she looked up and asked, "Anything new at rehearsals?"

I said that one of the actors had had an accident.

"Poor fellow," she replied. "I hope he's alright."

I went on to explain that he was in the hospital with two broken legs and wasn't expected to be able to play the part of Iago.

"What a shame," she said and went back to her cooking. Ben and Leah didn't bother to look up from their work but you could feel a sense of "nothing is going to get in our way and don't you forget it, mister."

It was time to pay the rent on all the places and Ben had
Ariela drive me up to Blainville the next day. The truck was
parked in the yard, and there was smoke rising from the
farmhouse chimney. Ariela drove up to the front door and
got out and let me slide behind the wheel. It was the first time
I was allowed to drive a vehicle in weeks. There was a definite
chain of command here which I accepted, and I was definitely
on the bottom. I then drove next door to the old farmer's
house and paid him the rent. I could tell he was a little miffed
at the comings and goings at the farmhouse but with the
language barrier I just smiled and left him with the money.

I drove back to the farmhouse and walked in the door
to a scene almost identical to the apartment I was staying
at in Montreal. There were pictures pinned up on the wall
and maps spread out on the table and three team members
I hadn't seen since Tel Aviv busy reading transcripts and
studying pictures. At that point I could tell the hunt was on
but there was no prey in our sites.

We drove back to Montreal and stopped first at the
apartment where Ariela was staying and this time we both
went to the landlord's office and paid the rent. You could see
he had as big a crush on her as I did and they talked in French
while I stood around. We then went into the apartment and it
was the same as the other two lodgings, team members busy
doing exactly the same thing. After a short stay we drove back
to the first apartment where we received our orders for the
rest of the day.

Ben had a particular interest in the same three
establishments, only today he added a fourth, a dry cleaner
on the same street as the other places. I had nothing to have
dry cleaned so Leah and Ariela packed up their dry cleaning
and had me schlep it down to the car.

When I got back to the apartment the two girls were sitting
at the table reading a transcript and giggling. I immediately
realized that the dry cleaners was a joke and had nothing to
do with the mission.

"I'm not fuckin' stupid, you know," I said, really feeling like an errand boy only to get one of those looks from Ben that sent the officer-to-enlisted-man message that I understood very clearly.

My little show of temperament didn't stop the girls from giggling and I heard one of them say something that sounded like "Der Shvartsa is Shtupping der Shicksa," and then Ben even joined in the laughter. I could tell they were speaking Yiddish from hearing it on the kibbutz but didn't know what they were saying.

Ariela explained to me that the director of the play was having an affair with the leading lady who was married to someone else and it should make for an interesting outcome. She also went on to tell me I must start working at making people like me. She said the transcripts indicated that the director was leaning toward me as a replacement for the injured actor but he wasn't happy and had been putting in phone calls to try to avoid that.

"Why do you think people don't like me?" I asked her and she told me to go and look in the mirror.

"It's in your eyes," she said. "You scare people."

"Well, then, I should make a perfect Iago," I said. "Except for the faggy part."

At the next rehearsal the other candidates who the director would have preferred to read for the part respectfully declined and he had to entertain me for the part. And while the rest of the cast read their parts he took me aside to read with him. I'm sure he had to be a little impressed with me as the part of Iago is actually bigger than the part of Othello and I began to see how the relationship between the two parts actually resembled reality. At the end of that night he announced he had picked his cast and I had won the part. He then announced he was having flyers printed up to advertise the play and asked for volunteers to distribute them around the city. I immediately volunteered to hand them out to all the businesses in the area.

My routine with the team didn't change, only now I had flyers for the play to deliver, an excuse to enter any establishment that Ben wanted to send me into. I took possession of a large stack of them the next evening and scored a few points with the director.

When the team met the next day Ben had the map out on the table and had certain areas he wanted me to canvass with the flyers. He went over how I was supposed to act when I went into the businesses. It was all going to be a little crazy, he explained, because most would be French and the ones that were not would be Arabic. He then joked that I would be lucky to interest anyone in the play but that didn't matter. We were narrowing down the area where our targets were hiding and it shouldn't be long before we would be on to them. Ben also had several apartment complexes he wanted me to deliver the flyers to and wanted me to bang on some doors.

I hadn't given it any thought before but I began to wonder what I was going to do if things all came together and we accomplished our mission before we put on the play. Was I still going to stick around for this ridiculous play that I had absolutely no interest in or would I disappear with the rest of the team? I also wondered if Ben would have an unexpected surprise for me.

The more I read over the play the more I began to understand what true evil really was. During the day I was on the hunt for some people with the intention of killing them and at night I was acting out the part of a man who was truly a devil. I was becoming exhausted and getting close to burnout stage.

Ben had me hand out my first package of flyers on the street that included the restaurant, the bakery, and the food store. I know it made me feel different having a reason to be in that part of the city but the only person that even gave the flyer a good look was the queer waiter and he immediately taped it up in his window.

When I got back to the apartment there was a different feeling than at any other time. Ben was packing up his suitcase and the team leaders were all sitting around looking like they were waiting for orders. Ben spoke to them in Hebrew and then focused his attention on me. He called me over to the kitchen table that had been cleared of all their maps and photos that usually cluttered it and asked me to sit down. "I have been recalled to Tel Aviv," he said. "There is new and vital information concerning our targets and I will be gone for about a week."

He then went on to tell me that a phone call placed from the restaurant to a number in Libya had set off red lights throughout the entire intelligence community.

He then handed me an envelope full of money and instructed me to dress up in my fancy duds and at the next rehearsal to invite the cast of the play to dinner at the restaurant. I said there were about fifteen or sixteen players and it would look a little funny me being able to afford such a thing. Usually the ever serious Ben, using his best New York accent, looked me in the eyes and said, "It's show time, kid. Tell them anything, you inherited a bunch of money, I don't care, just make a big splash."

Leah, seeing my nervousness, sat down and said, "Here's the perfect time to learn how to make people like you. Just start spreading money around and you will soon have lots of friends." I could see the looks of the team leaders; their eyes were all on me. We had entered the last phase of our mission and now it was my turn to become an actor on the stage and in real life.

The next day Ariela dropped me off near the restaurant as usual only this time when I went in I asked the queer waiter if I could speak to the manager. When he returned he asked if I had a problem. He was quite happy when I asked to make reservations for sixteen people, explaining to him that we were the group that was advertised in the flyer that he had already taken down from his window. He was very obsequious and said that it was all a mistake and he would be happy to put it back if I could supply him with another copy. He was very nice and as I walked back to the car I wondered if I would be allowed to kill this guy. Then I thought, "Him and the waiter both; that would be a good day's work."

That evening as I entered the theatre the cast took note of the country yokel in the fancy clothes. Some of the other cast members wore suits and ties all the time but it was the first time for me and it really made a difference. The director was always dressed impeccably and he commented on my new appearance. It was even more pleasing to the group when I invited them all to dine with me after rehearsal. I could hear Leah's words in the back of my head about making friends and I was sure I had found the key.

Rehearsal went by very well and even one of the young ladies who were playing a minor role began to flirt with me a little bit. The director, noticing my new status, joked to me out of earshot of the rest of the cast, "There's a little bit of crumpet for you if you're interested."

On our way to the restaurant I rode alone with the director in his Cadillac. He came from money so he appreciated my gesture and he even opened up to me during the car ride. "You know, you weren't my first choice for the part," he said. "I just didn't think you would be able to pull it off, I thought you were too young and too unsophisticated but maybe I was wrong." His words didn't sit all that well with me but I knew he was right.

The entire cast met at the restaurant and the manager had several tables placed together to accommodate our group. I told them to order what they wished and asked for the wine list. I had been forbidden by Leah to drink anything but ignored the order. I felt that there was no way I could screw anything up this evening. When the first bottles of wine came, the director offered a toast and everyone joined in.

For a bunch of people who seemed to be stuffed shirts they could really party. We drank copious amounts of wine and ate our fill. As the cast became more merry, we would take turns reciting our parts mixed in with operatic arias by some of the ladies and the director, who was a singer as well as an actor. They were all impressed when I joined the director in a song from Pagliacci, in perfect Italian, with a full tenor flourish.

All in all everyone was full of food and drink and I was the drunkest of all. I had completely forgotten why I was there in the first place and didn't take note of any of the waiters who were serving us. When it came time to pay the bill I pulled out my bank roll like it was nothing, paid the bill, and left a big tip as I had been instructed to by Ben. It was the only thing I had remembered to do that evening.

The director dropped me off in front of the apartment that evening and I staggered up the stairs and let myself in. I was so drunk that I never noticed that the apartment had gone through an overhaul. Gone were the photos pinned to the wall. Also gone were the stacks of documents and transcripts in several languages. The place was in fact looking normal.

When I woke up in the morning I was sick but not alone. Yonnie was cooking breakfast and had a great belly laugh as I rushed to the bathroom to heave. Leah was also stirring around when I returned from the bathroom. She poured me a coffee and commented on what a party it was.

At rehearsal that evening I wasn't the only actor who was feeling the effects of the night before. But generally I was the flavour of the week and we managed to struggle through the evening. I was now everyone's friend, the rich kid from out west who didn't work but had money to burn.

Before we broke that night the director announced that we were starting to look like an acting troupe but had a tremendous amount of ground to cover and would have to meet every evening until our first dress rehearsal.

When I returned to the apartment I could feel things were a lot looser. With Ben away Leah announced there were no assignments to run the next day and we were going shopping. "You must have another outfit," she said. "Orders."

I was then instructed to invite the cast out to eat again but this time to try to keep my wits about me and study every face in the restaurant. I asked if it could wait a couple of days as I was still feeling the effects of the last party.

When I showed up at rehearsal the next night with a new suit and announced another party the crowd erupted in applause. It was a lot of work for an amateur theatrical group and this gesture was really appreciated. I may have outwardly been believable but inside I was feeling the strain and starting to experience a paranoia partly brought on by my dual life, the evil character I was playing, and maybe just a pang of conscience that up until now had been absent from my personality.

After rehearsal we all met at the same restaurant and went through the same kind of celebration. Everyone was loud and I even ended up making out with one of the actresses in the washroom. I was starting to lose any control I might have had but no one seemed to mind. "The Show Must Go On!" I heard the director shout as I appeared out of the washroom with the actress in tow.

The next day I woke up again with a terrible hangover. I began to look through the cupboards for a pain killer for my headache when I opened up one cupboard and inside was Ben's revolver and his automatic. He had obviously left them behind and I picked up the .45 and handled it with care. I checked it for ammunition and when I was satisfied it was loaded and without giving it a thought I placed it in my belt. I then went through the rest of the cupboards. I found some aspirin, swallowed half a dozen, and went back to sleep on the couch.

I was allowed to sleep all day then Leah had me up and showered and off to rehearsal again that night. She said that she had heard from Ben and the original intelligence we had about the restaurant was premature, our targets were not there yet but were expected to show up as kitchen workers. That meant more parties for me; I was going to be a permanent fixture there even if I was turning into a drunken fool.

We were now only a couple of weeks away from our first dress rehearsal and I was getting more paranoid by the day. I managed to keep it from the team because Ben was away and Ariela hadn't been around for over a week. I could also keep my mental breakdown from the cast but in reality I was losing control. I began to carry the automatic to rehearsals and went through fantasies of shooting the whole cast and then I thought, "Why don't I just go into the restaurant and shoot everyone in there? Surely I'll get the right people." I was becoming psychotic but the drink kept me going.

The last two weeks of rehearsal were exhausting but the cast were up to it. As intense as the team was in their hunt, the cast had to apply the same kind of energy to put on the show; whereas they were worlds apart, they were both tragedies that were about to collide. I was instructed to invite the cast out to another party.

Before I knew it the day of the dress rehearsal was on us. Hundreds of letters had been sent out to the local patrons of the arts and tickets had been sold. The cast and crew were ready. I showed up early for the dress rehearsal, pulled the .45 out of my belt and placed it in my locker, then went for my costume fitting and makeup. I would only need my sword on this night, I thought.

The director was busy going over last minute details with the crew while the cast scurried about dealing with their last minute jitters. The young lady who was playing Bianca, who I had been sparking with ever since our drunken tryst in the washroom of the restaurant, came up to me and in a bundle of nerves sought my comfort. Not since I had first tasted combat had I felt so alive. The sound of the crowd beginning to enter the auditorium took me back to the first time I had heard the roar of artillery. I could hear the thump of the helicopter blades and the "lock and load" order as we were approaching a hot LZ. I began to gasp for breath as my heart was pounding.

It must have been quite a scene holding onto Bianca when the director came by and gave me a friendly pat on the back. "Break a leg, Iago. I'm counting on you," he said. He then went around to everyone like a gunnery sergeant rallying the rest of the nervous cast. He was a true professional and this was his moment.

Once the lights went down and the play began everyone lost their nervousness and we all performed to the best of our ability. There were a few glitches as expected at a dress rehearsal but all in all we pulled it off. When the play was over and we stood before the audience for our curtain call something happened to me. It was another epiphany. The applause did something to me. I completely snapped. I remained on stage until there was no more clapping. Already suffering from a post traumatic delusionary attack the applause intensified my situation. Once backstage I invited everyone for a celebration at the only place I knew and we all loaded into cars and headed to the restaurant.

The staff at the restaurant were inviting as usual and our raucous behavior was tolerated. I ordered wine and we all toasted one another in a celebration of life. We ate and drank and laughed, and in my drunken state I forgot how I got there and even why I was there.

When I was returned to the apartment I was drunk and unruly and made a ruckus on my entry but anyone who was there didn't bother to show their displeasure. They let me fall on the couch to sleep it off.

When I woke up the next morning I was in pain and sick as a dog. Leah was the first to give me a little comfort. She made an herbal tea and had me sip it and wash down some pain medication. Even in my state I could tell that things had changed. The atmosphere was tense. "Ben will be back today," Leah said, "and you better straighten yourself up." I heard her but had such a headache that I couldn't respond.

I lay on the couch until late in the afternoon, when I woke up from dozing off to see Ben standing in front of the couch looking at me. "You're doing a good job, Kanook," he said. "But now the real show is about to start."

I rolled over to try to go back to sleep but then he kicked my feet and ordered me to get up. Ben then said to me, "We have to drive up to the farm for a meeting and what have you done with my gun?"

It was still in my belt and, not quite sober yet, I said, "It's right here. Come and get it if you dare," and I reached for my belt.

Ben backed off and stood looking at me and screamed, "Get up, you crazy fucking shegetz!"

That was all I needed and I got up and walked to the bathroom still retaining possession of the firearm.

Leah was the only other person in the apartment at the time and as I walked past her I could see she was trying to pretend this wasn't happening, but I was sure that if I reached for the gun she would have dropped me before I could shoot Ben. I showered and shaved and changed out of my suit and walked back into the living room and apologized to both of them. Ben wasn't impressed but in his absolute professional manner acted as if nothing had happened. The only thing he said as we left the apartment was, "Are you going to hand over that gun or not?"

All I said in reply was, "Nope."

We drove out of Montreal and into the country, arriving at the farm in the late afternoon. All the cars were parked in the yard, even the pickup truck. When we walked into the house the place was silent. The whole team was there and I could smell a familiar cigarette smoke that I hadn't smelled since Tel Aviv. I knew instantly who smoked that brand. He was sitting at the kitchen table and when we walked into the room he got up from his chair and walked over to me, looked me straight in the eyes, and offered me his hand. I shook it like a man and everything up till then started to make sense. He then motioned me over to the kitchen table and lying on the table were two pictures, one of a man and one of a woman.

"Do you recognize these people?" he asked me. And I replied that I didn't. Then he went on and said that after tonight's performance I was to invite everyone out to dinner again and I was forbidden to drink any wine at all. I was instructed to make a trip to the washroom and then make what would appear to be a wrong turn and enter the kitchen and make a positive identification. There would be no room for error.

He went on to remind me that the whole mission was now to depend on me. We could not make any mistakes. I was then told to study the pictures on my way back to the city. He then instructed Ariela to drive me back to Montreal while he and the rest of the team stayed behind to plan the next phase of the operation. I know he noticed the .45 in my belt but unlike Ben he didn't ask for it.

"So you have been cheating on me?" was the first thing Ariela said to me as we drove out of the farm yard.

"Fuck you," I replied, and we drove the rest of the way back to Montreal in silence.

CHAPTER THIRTEEN

The dress rehearsal was now behind us and tonight there would be members of the press and a full house, and the atmosphere was electric. I had mixed feelings about who I was and what I was. I wanted a drink so bad but even though Ben may have frightened me, "He" had instilled in me a sense of meaning and purpose. Ben was just a young gun like me but "He" was someone important and must have had the ear of people right at the top. I wondered at that moment if Golda, whose speech that October day had changed my life forever, knew we were here and might have actually known that I existed. It was just about too much to handle but I soldiered on, afraid I might forget my lines or, even worse, screw up at the restaurant after the performance.

The lights dimmed for a second time and we all performed our hearts out. When the audience gave us a round of applause at the end of the performance I drank it up like the alcohol I was craving, forgetting for the moment my true purpose for being there in the first place. After the bows and curtain calls I again invited the entire cast for a meal of celebration and we all trooped off to the restaurant for another celebration.

Once in the restaurant I ordered wine but was very abstemious. We laughed and ate and sang and had the whole place in our laps. The event was so raucous that no one noticed when I or anyone else went to the washroom.

I did exactly as I was ordered to do. When I made my trip to the washroom I pretended to be drunk, which was not out of character, and made the wrong turn into the kitchen. I stumbled around and was immediately approached by the queer waiter who by now knew me as a preferred customer and calmed down the kitchen staff. Before he could usher me out I did have a chance to look around and there they were staring me right in the face. I was close enough to touch them and they looked exactly as they did in the pictures. I had seen all I needed to.

It was all I could do not to pull out my .45 and start blasting away, but for once I was able to follow orders and I allowed the queer waiter to escort me back to the dining area and to the party.

I didn't know how I felt and had to have a drink to calm down. I was shaking when I put the first glass of wine to my lips and couldn't stop drinking until I was drunk. At the end of dinner I paid the bill and over-tipped the waiters and got my usual come-on by the queer waiter and left the restaurant. I decided to walk home that night and begged off a ride from the director knowing I had better sober up before I arrived back at the apartment.

I hadn't walked far before a car pulled up and I was ordered in. It was Ben and Ariela and the debriefing began immediately. Ben didn't bother to scream at me for drinking, they just wanted to know what I had seen and after I confirmed what they had been pretty certain of we all drove back to the apartment in silence. I was half drunk and starting to fall asleep in the back seat of the car when I spoke out loud, "I guess it's checkmate for those two fuckers, *eh!*" emphasizing Canada's most noted colloquialism. "I'll kill 'em both for you tomorrow night. I just need a little sleep right now." My drunken outburst was met with silence and I slept the rest of the way back to the apartment.

I woke up on the couch the next morning and Ben, Leah, and Ariela were sitting at the kitchen table drinking coffee. It took a few minutes to remember the events of the previous night. I was just happy not to be too hung over. The three of them were very calm. Ben, in an out of character way, said to me, "When you're ready we have some things to go over."

"Just let me shake out the cobwebs and I'll be right with you," I said, and went into the bathroom to take a shower. There was going to be no hurry on this day; this was to be a day of death, the grim reaper was about to come calling. I wondered while I was showering if they were going to let me do it or did they have some other plan.

When I finished my shower I walked into the kitchen and asked Ben matter-of-factly, "So, how are we going to do this?"

He was all business as usual and said that I wasn't going to do anything except go to my performance and then invite the whole cast back to the restaurant one more time. "You are going to go through exactly the same routine as last night except you will phone this number at exactly midnight and report if they are in the restaurant or not. We will take care of the rest."

"That's all, eh?" I said. "Well, that should be no problem. I could take care of this if you wanted me to, you know that."

Ben then said that they had a plan and it would be carried out as ordered and that was final. I was relieved and disappointed at the same time. I wanted to show these people what I could do and that I wasn't just their bum boy, but orders were orders, and if I had learned anything in the military it was that a soldier's only worth was his ability to carry out orders. I filled up a coffee cup and sat down with the three of them and there didn't seem like there was much else to say.

Ben produced a stack of bills and handed it to me. "Midnight," he said several times, "you be on that phone and don't you fuck up."

I got the message loud and clear and went back and lay down on the couch and went to sleep. I slept for a good part of the day and then got up and ate something and began to prepare for the evening's performance.

When I arrived at the theatre everything seemed normal. The cast and crew were milling about but after a couple of shows no one was as nervous as the previous days.

There was a man standing at the stage door and he asked me if I had a minute to talk.

I said, "No problem," but I was very cautious, thinking today's the day, and wondered what could happen next. He handed me his card and as it turned out he was a producer from Stratford, Ontario, and he offered me a job sweeping floors and emptying ashtrays at Canada's premier Shakespeare festival. He said I could get some real training and experience and make a career out of acting. He said he thought I had potential. I was dumbfounded, took his card, and promised to get back to him after we finished our run here in Montreal. That helped to take my mind off what was really happening that day but it didn't take away from the events that were planned for that evening.

When the lights went down and everyone performed their hearts out, my heart was not really in my acting. I struggled through the night but without any real passion. The director even made a comment between scenes. "Come on, Iago," he said. "Put some effort into it."

As was getting to be a habit I invited everyone to dine after the performance, and the entire cast and crew filed out of the theatre into their cars and drove to the restaurant. I traveled with the director and Bianca, who was by now acting toward me as I was acting toward Ariela. Now I could understand why Ariela was turned off by my behavior.

I had my hand resting on my .45 as I sat in the Cadillac and we drove across the city. I was going to be ready if something went awry. When we approached the restaurant I looked around the deserted streets for anything unusual and noticed the pickup truck parked in the back alley behind the restaurant. I also noticed one of the cars I had purchased parked across the street from the building that housed the restaurant. When I saw these vehicles I knew then that it was going to be "Show Time In Montreal."

The maitre d' welcomed us en masse as before. He liked the money I was throwing around even if we were an unruly bunch. He didn't, however, have a clue what his restaurant was in for on this night.

We started drinking and toasting as before and I never missed a toast. I felt that this was probably the last time this was going to occur so I intended to have a good time. As I became drunker and the time got closer to midnight I did my washroom exit and wrong turn move as I had been instructed to. As I entered the kitchen they were there, the two of them, one washing dishes and the other preparing food.

"Hey," I said, "I used to be a dish washer," and staggered back out of the kitchen.

At precisely midnight I made my way to the pay telephone, put in the dime, and dialed the number. Yonnie answered the call and all I said was, "It's a go," and hung up and went back to the party. At this point the director stood up and made a toast to his beloved Desdemona and suggested that our next play be a comedy instead of a tragedy and suggested we perform "All's Well That Ends Well."

I had never heard of this play before but I thought how appropriate and began to drink harder. I was becoming very drunk at this point and after the director proposed another toast I said to him, "Do you want to see some comedy?" and he replied sure. I then got up and called over the queer waiter and made him stand against the wall and place a bottle of wine on his head. "Just stand here," I said. "This won't hurt a bit." I then walked back to my seat and sat down. As the rest of the cast began to take notice I pulled my .45 out of my belt and fired a shot at the waiter.

The bottle of wine exploded on the waiter's head, he fainted and dropped like a stone. The loud noise of the gun going off silenced the whole restaurant and everyone thought I had shot the waiter. The director then jumped up and shouted out, "It's only a stage prop! It's only a stage prop!" and the crowd roared with laughter.

Desdemona, thinking something untoward had occurred, ran to the queer waiter and began to wipe the wine away from his face. The manager came rushing over to the table and I pulled out my wad of bills and handed him a hundred dollars. He took the money but wasn't impressed and said he was calling the police. I didn't care and told him to go ahead.

I then took the gun out of my belt, pushed the release mechanism, and dropped the magazine onto the floor. I then handed it over to the director who handled it with an unusual curiosity. He then passed it on and everyone who was interested began to observe the weapon.

By this time the waiter had regained consciousness and came over to the table and began putting on a little show of temperament. I again pulled out my wad of bills and handed him a hundred dollars, and he took the money. It was probably more than he made in a week but he was still not satisfied.

We were so drunk by this time we didn't notice the restaurant empty of the other patrons and fill up with Montreal's finest with guns drawn and pointing at us. Before we knew it we were all lined up against the same wall that was covered with red wine and sporting a big hole from the projectile.

A police sergeant then stood in front of the cast and crew of "Othello" holding up the .45 and questioned us all, one at a time, and everyone repeated the same line, "I thought it was a stage prop, I thought it was a stage prop," over and over again. No one ratted me off and I concurred with the rest of the cast that "I thought it was a stage prop."

The manager knew differently but even he gave me a reprieve and said he didn't know who fired the shot. The thing that made him the maddest, though, was the fact that he lost his entire kitchen staff. It seemed those that weren't terrorists were illegals and they all made a mad dash for the back door. Unfortunately for two of them they were in for a little surprise.

The director gave me a ride home that night, and I staggered up the stairs, fumbled with my key in the lock, somehow letting myself in the door, flopping on the bed and passing out.

I woke up the next morning with a pounding headache and rushed to the bathroom and got sick. I then began drinking out of the water tap in the sink to try to quench my thirst and get the awful taste out of my mouth. While I was doing this the events of the previous evening started to flow through my mind. "Oh shit," I said out loud, "I'll bet I'm in trouble now."

I then sheepishly walked out into the front room. My head was still pounding, and Leah was standing there with a glass of water and some pain pills which she offered to me and I accepted. I washed the pills down with the water and handed her back the glass. I was expecting to be excoriated by her or anyone but she just walked back to the kitchen table, sat down, and resumed drinking her coffee. She appeared to be reading the paper. "How did the performance go last night?" she asked very nonchalantly.

I replied that we had another full house. Then I asked, "How about you?"

She replied, "The same," without looking up from her paper. She then said, "I think Ariela and I would like to come and see you perform tonight. Can you get us some tickets?"

"Ya, sure, how many would you like?"

"I'll let you know," she said. Then she asked how my headache was and I told her it was going away. "That's good," she replied. "If you need any more medication just let me know." I walked back to the couch and lay down and went back to sleep.

That evening when I walked into the theatre the cast and crew were in a jovial mood. No one had ever been through an evening like that before. It was just one joke after another and rolling laughter. I was asked if we were going to the restaurant after the performance and I just laughed, saying that I needed a night off.

When the lights went down that evening and we took to the stage I looked out into the audience and there in the front row sat the entire team. Even "He" was sitting there. I was never that nervous before and I played my heart out. As the play got underway I even ad-libbed a little bit during one of the sword fighting scenes and slapped one of the ladies on her ass and gave her a wink, to her horror. I could see that the director wasn't impressed but by now he knew I was a loose cannon and seemed resigned to that. When the play was over and we went back on stage for our curtain call I could see the team all on their feet applauding. I was moved beyond words.

Backstage I announced to the director and cast that tonight there wouldn't be a party, that I was going home early, and they all understood. The director asked if I needed a ride and I begged off telling him I was going to walk home and I would see him the next night.

After getting out of my costume I exited out of the stage door. Sitting in the parking lot was one of the cars I had purchased for the team and I walked over to it. Ben was behind the wheel and he rolled down the window. "Ya want a ride?" he asked.

"Not if you're going to whack me out," I joked.

"Don't be silly," he said. "Hop in."

I climbed into the car and he asked me if I was hungry. I said, "Would it matter?"

"How come you're in such a bad mood?" he said.

"I don't fuckin' trust you, that's why," I replied.

"That's good, that's good," he said, and we drove off.

We drove across Montreal and parked in front of a little French restaurant, got out of the car, and walked into the place. Already seated was the entire team, including "Him."

He motioned for me to come and sit next to him and said, "Congratulations, I saw your performance tonight and really enjoyed it." That broke the ice and then he asked Ariela to order for us. "She speaks French, you know," he said, making some small talk. I had never seen the whole team together before and for anybody who didn't know us we could have been the local bowling club out for an evening after the lanes had shut down.

There was no mention of what we were about, but in the back of my mind I thought there were probably a couple of unmarked graves somewhere up in the Laurentian Mountains that would go unnoticed for eternity.

"So what are you going to do after you finish your run with this play?" he asked as we ate our meal. I then told him that I had been offered a job at the Stratford Festival and he listened intently. "You know, I hope you don't mind me saying this," he said, "but I don't really think you are cut out for sweeping floors and hoping for a big break in Hollywood."

"Have you got anything better?" I replied.

"Yes, I do," was his answer. He then pulled out a business card in Hebrew block letters that I couldn't understand and wrote a name on the back of it. Then he said, "We have some openings for some instructors in South America. It seems they want to get a nice little revolution going on down there and someone with your talents would fit right in."

He went on to say, "I don't think you belong on the stage. I think you belong back in the jungle. I hope you don't mind me saying this, but you are one crazy Kanook." He then handed me the card. "If you present this at the embassy in Bogotá they will set you up. They will be waiting to hear from you."

I accepted the card, looked at it, and turned it over and read the name on the back that meant nothing to me. The name was in Spanish and it read, "Pablo Escobar."

"Who's this guy?" I asked.

"Oh, he's just a guy who's trying to make a living down there," was his reply.

"OK," I said, "I'll think about it."

There was no wine served at this meal and when we finished eating and were preparing to leave one by one the team either shook my hand, or in the case of Ariela and Leah, gave me a big hug and a kiss. After Ben shook my hand he handed me the keys to the car he was driving. He told me the rest of the vehicles were parked up at the farm and I could sell them off to get a little traveling money. We then walked out of the restaurant; everyone left by Montreal taxi cabs.

As Ben's cab was starting to roll he called out to me, "Hey, I'll see you in Bogotá," and I just smiled and waved goodbye.

And there I was standing on the side of the street wondering if this had really happened.

The play ran for another two weeks until the audiences began to dwindle and the only time the cast went out on a party again was on the director's dime after our last performance. I was alone in the apartment and began to crave some action. I began to wake up without the awful hangovers and soon realized I wasn't interested in going to Stratford. Then I took all the vehicles back to the old man at the dealership and went to the library to find an atlas. Twice I had climbed aboard airplanes without having a clue where I was destined and this time wouldn't be the third. I looked for South America on the map and then found Colombia. I then took my Canadian passport to the airport and bought a ticket to Bogotá.

As the jet taxied out onto the runway I thought about all that had gone on in the last year and wondered what would happen in the coming year but that's another story for another time.

"Homeward you think we must be sailing to our own land; no, elsewhere is the voyage"
The Odyssey Homer

Acknowledgements

To the approximately 40,000 Canadians who voluntarily joined and served beside their brothers and sisters of the U.S. Armed Forces and especially those 103 names that appear on the wall in Washington, D.C.

Foreign Enlistment Act:
- *Any person, who being a Canadian national, whether within or residing outside Canada voluntarily accepts or agrees to accept any commission or engagement in the armed forces of any foreign state at war with any friendly state.... is guilty of an offense of this act.*

At the time Vietnam was considered a friendly state by Canada (*very ironic since they allowed and encouraged the business sector to manufacture and supply war materials to <u>South Vietnam</u> and the Canadian government itself supplied over 27 million dollars in financial aid to <u>South Vietnam</u>*), making it illegal to serve in the U.S. Armed Forces. However, the U.S. military found a loophole in the act and accepted volunteers from Canada. The biggest downfall to the Canadians who volunteered was the fact that they had to list a U.S. city or town as place of birth. After the war, there were no records of Canadians who had served in the U.S. Armed Forces in Vietnam. However, through extensive and painfully slow research, some but not all of these volunteers were identified. Unfortunately, we may never know exactly how many have not been found and /or accounted for.